PRAISE FOR TAMMY L. GRACE

"I had planned on an early night but couldn't put this book down until I finished it around 3am. Like her other books, this one features fascinating characters with a plot that mimics real life in the best way. My recommendation: it's time to read every book Tammy L Grace has written."
— *Carolyn, review of Beach Haven*

"*A Season of Hope* is a perfect holiday read! Warm wonderful and gentle tale reflecting small town romance at its best."
— *Jeanie, review of A Season for Hope: A Christmas Novella*

"This book is a clean, simple romance with a background story very similar to the works of Debbie Macomber. If you like Macomber's books you will like this one. The main character, Hope and her son Jake are on a road trip when their car breaks down, thus starts the story. A holiday tale filled with dogs, holiday fun, and the joy of giving will warm your heart.

reveals their hidden secrets—an absorbing page-turning read."
— *Jason Deas, bestselling author of Pushed and Birdsongs*

"I could not put this book down! It was so well written & a suspenseful read! This is definitely a 5-star story! I'm hoping there will be a sequel!"
—*Colleen, review of Killer Music*

"This is the best book yet by this author. The plot was well crafted with an unanticipated ending. I like to try to leap ahead and see if I can accurately guess the outcome. I was able to predict some of the plot but not the actual details which made reading the last several chapters quite engrossing."

—*0001PW, review of Deadly Connection*

DEADLY DECEPTION

DEADLY DECEPTION

COOPER HARRINGTON DETECTIVE NOVELS

BOOK 5

TAMMY L. GRACE

LONE MOUNTAIN PRESS

DEADLY DECEPTION
A novel by
Tammy L. Grace

www.tammylgrace.com
Facebook: https://www.facebook.com/tammylgrace.books
Twitter: @TammyLGrace

Published in the United States by Lone Mountain Press, Nevada

ISBN 978-1-945591-69-3 (paperback)
ISBN 978-1-945591-68-6 (eBook)
FIRST EDITION
Cover by Elizabeth Mackey Graphic Design
Printed in the United States of America

ALSO BY TAMMY L. GRACE

GLASS BEACH COTTAGE SERIES

Beach Haven

Moonlight Beach

Beach Dreams

WRITING AS CASEY WILSON

A Dog's Hope

A Dog's Chance

WISHING TREE SERIES

The Wishing Tree

Wish Again

Overdue Wishes

SISTERS OF THE HEART SERIES

Greetings from Lavender Valley

Pathway to Lavender Valley

Sanctuary at Lavender Valley

Blossoms at Lavender Valley

Comfort in Lavender Valley

Reunion in Lavender Valley

Remember to subscribe to Tammy's exclusive group of readers for your gift, only available to readers on her mailing list. **Sign up at www.tammylgrace.com. Follow this link to subscribe at https://wp.me/P9umIy-e** and you'll receive the exclusive interview she did with all the canine characters in her Hometown Harbor Series.

Follow Tammy on Facebook by liking her page. You may also follow Tammy on book retailers or at BookBub by clicking on the follow button.

For Aunt Vicki, one of my biggest fans and supporters who shares my love for Coop & Gus

CHAPTER ONE

Coop smiled as he concentrated on the dark elixir streaming from the coffeepot Myrtle held over his oversized cup. He added sugar to his cup and shoved his empty plate to the edge of the table. The maple pecan pancakes studded with bits of candied bacon hit the spot, and he was stuffed.

Ben was on the phone and when he disconnected, he reached for the check. "Gotta run. It's been a long week, and my hopes for a quiet Friday aren't looking good." He slid out of the booth. "We'll miss you tomorrow night."

"Trust me, I'd much rather be at the stadium watching the Sounds instead of at another one of Aunt Camille's charity events."

"It makes her happy and for all she does for you, you can suck it up once in a while."

"I'm sure I could get you in." Coop wiggled his brows at his old friend.

Ben chuckled and held up a hand. "I try to stay as far away from that crowd as possible. Too many politicians and bazillionaires for me. I'll stick with my kind at the baseball game."

"Count me and Dad in for the next home game." Coop took the takeout box Myrtle delivered and thanked her.

Ben was driving away by the time Coop climbed behind the wheel of his Jeep. Gus stared at the takeout box and drooled as Coop steered the Jeep from Peg's Pancakes to his office, only a few minutes away.

As Coop pulled into the parking area behind the charming brick house that served as his office, he glanced over at Gus. Coop reached for a rag from the backseat and wiped the pool of dog drool from the edge of the passenger seat. "I know AB's breakfast smells delicious. Don't worry, pal; she'll share it with you."

He admired the purple blooms of the redbud trees along the back of the house and carried the takeout box, with Gus at his heels. After a quick stop in the kitchen for a cup of decaf, he wandered to AB's desk. "Gus wants you to know he's a huge fan of blueberries, and they're a superfood, and you wouldn't want to put his health at risk by not sharing your pancakes with him."

She smiled and reached out to rub the sweet dog's ears. Coop chuckled at the look of pure adoration on Gus' face, his tongue sliding out of his mouth as he soaked in the attention from his favorite gal pal.

As she massaged his ears, AB gazed at Gus with the same love in her eyes. "Don't you worry. I'll give you a few bites. You're the best dog ever, aren't you?"

Gus' tail thumped against the wood floor.

With his loyal dog ignoring him for AB's charms, Coop shuffled to his office. He took a sip of his coffee, wrinkled his nose, and set it on the coaster AB insisted he use. Happy he'd had a few cups of the real brew at Peg's this morning, he dug into the files on his desk.

With their recent few days off in sunny Florida, Coop was behind on a few things and determined to catch up by the end of the day. While he was reviewing reports, Gus wandered into his office and climbed onto the leather chair he used as his throne, where he promptly shut his eyes.

As Gus sighed, Coop shook his head. "Like he's had such a tough morning working hard to pay bills."

After several hours with his nose to the grindstone and few interruptions, Coop leaned back in his chair with the smile of accomplishment on his face. The stack of files was done and on AB's desk for billing or next steps. It was only three o'clock as he logged off his computer.

"Gus, I think we deserve an early out today and a walk in the park."

At one of his favorite words, Gus leapt from the chair and rushed over to Coop, tail wagging at high speed.

While Coop straightened his desk, AB came through the door, cradling a cup in her hands. She slid into the seat in front of Coop's desk. "I get the feeling somebody is taking off early?" She raised her brows at him.

"Gus and I are heading to the park."

"We're on for tomorrow, right? You're not going to try to find an excuse to skip the gala and sneak off to the baseball game?"

He rolled his eyes. "I'd love to find an excuse, but with Dad and Aunt Camille excited about it, not to mention you, I'm stuck. Arthur and Victoria are two of Aunt Camille's oldest friends, and it's for a good cause."

"It might be fun."

"A murder mystery, really? And black tie to boot. Aunt Camille already told me not to show off and solve it right off the bat. She said the fun is in the game, and I just need to play along. The only saving grace is the open bar."

"It's for charity. I'm looking forward to seeing that house and their estate."

"You mean chateau, right? It's a doozie."

"Coming from a girl with no social life, I'm looking forward to a night out and a chance to dress up."

"As I recall, Ms. Davenport, Aunt Camille dragged us to a gala in January and went so far as to offer me up to be auctioned off. Ring a bell?"

AB flung her head back and laughed. "Yes, Counselor. I do recall and if I remember correctly, you later admitted you had fun."

He harrumphed and motioned for Gus to follow him. On his way to the door, he hollered, "See you at the house tomorrow, AB. Aunt Camille wants to leave by five thirty."

She followed him as far as the kitchen and rinsed her cup. "It'll be dope, trust me."

He turned and shook his head. "Dope? Really, AB?"

"Isn't that what the kids say now?" She laughed and waved goodbye.

CHAPTER TWO

Gus cocked his head from his vantage point in Coop's bedroom, where he sat watching him adjust his tuxedo. Coop caught Gus' look in the mirror and chuckled. "My thoughts exactly, Gus. What the heck am I doing?"

He turned from the mirror and adjusted the bow tie. "Aunt Camille is the only person who holds the power to make me do this. She's our world, and we'd do anything for her, right?"

Gus gave him a short bark of agreement. Coop reached out and petted his head. "I need to keep your golden glitter off this black suit."

Gus lowered his head to the cushion. "I know, but we won't be gone long. You can take a nap and by the time you wake up, we'll be home. I also think Aunt Camille has some bits of steak she's treating you to in your dinner bowl tonight. She feels guilty that you can't come with us."

Gus hurried from his chair and nosed the cracked door open before darting through it. Coop laughed as he slipped his phone, small notebook, and wallet inside his jacket pocket and wandered out to the kitchen.

When he arrived, he found Gus slurping up the last of the tiny bits of steak that clung to his bowl. Charlie walked up behind him. "Looking good, son. Looking good."

Coop turned and took in his dad, dressed in an almost identical tuxedo, except he was wearing a black and blue jacquard vest under his jacket. "Very dapper, Dad."

The tap of Aunt Camille's heels from her wing of the house announced her imminent arrival, and Coop lowered his voice. "You know we could be sitting behind third base right now with Ben?"

Charlie winked. "Anything that makes Camille happy is worth a small sacrifice. We can catch a game next week."

Coop gripped his dad's shoulder. "You're right, of course. I just hate fancy gatherings and even more so the group of phony people who will be there. Aunt Camille is a rare commodity. She's got a pure heart and genuinely cares about these charities and donates lots of her money and time to worthy causes. AB assures me it'll be fun, so I'll do my best to put on a happy face."

Charlie smiled at him. Then, his brows rose when Camille came around the corner, decked out in a flowing steely blue gown, adorned with subtle beads and sequins along the bodice. The color set off her fresh from the hairdresser white hair as she smiled at the two of them. "Gentlemen."

"Wow, Aunt Camille, you look like a million bucks." Coop grinned at the woman who was more like a mom to him than his actual mother.

Charlie nodded. "I agree. You're sure to be the belle of the ball."

Coop took a few photos of them on his phone, noting his

dad's vest matched her dress. Their happy smiles were worth wearing the tux.

The doorbell sounded. Coop turned away from the two of them. "That must be AB. I'll get it."

He hurried to the door, and his eyes widened. AB stood before him in a long shimmering gown in a champagne color. He stifled a gasp as he stared at the woman he worked next to each day. "Wow, AB. You're a total knockout."

She smiled and used her elbow to poke him in the ribs. "Shut your mouth, Coop, before you swallow a fly." She walked past him, her shimmering heels, in the same color as her dress, clicking across the floor.

After a few moments, Coop shut the door and his mouth. When he came into the kitchen, Camille was admiring the fabric of AB's dress, and his dad was grinning from ear to ear. He caught Coop's eye and winked. "I think the other ladies should just stay home tonight. These two are going to outshine everyone at this fancy soiree."

Coop nodded. "I couldn't agree more." He extended his arm to AB. "Shall we?"

As they made their way to the car, Camille stopped and insisted she take photos of Coop and AB and Coop with Charlie. Then, they all stood together, and Coop stretched out his hand to capture a selfie of the four of them.

With that done, he held the door for AB, while Charlie and Camille slipped into the backseat of Camille's Mercedes. Coop slid behind the wheel and set out for Sinclair Chateau as it was known, just a few miles from Camille's house.

The long driveway led to the sprawling estate, nestled in the trees and hidden from view. Valets in black and gold jackets were on hand to park cars and happily took the keys from Coop and gave him a claim ticket, while another one held the door and helped everyone out of the car.

They admired the trees wrapped with white twinkle lights as they climbed the stone steps to the massive entry doors, where a young woman in a sleek black dress took the tickets Camille offered and welcomed them to join the other guests in the Great Hall.

Coop's eyes widened as they stepped across a tiled floor into a huge space, furnished with round tables draped in black cloths, accented with gold napkins. Candles flickered among the crystal glasses and showy floral arrangements on each table. Women in sparkling gowns and men in black tuxedos milled about, sipping drinks or sitting at tables, chatting.

As soon as they arrived, a server offered them champagne or a Tennessee Stud from a tray or an alternative from the bar. The ladies took the flutes of champagne, and Charlie opted to pass even though he'd developed a taste for the popular drink made with bourbon and tea.

Coop held up his hand. "I'm the designated driver. How about an Arnold Palmer or just sweet tea, if you don't have that?"

Charlie nodded. "That sounds good to me, too."

"Right away," said the young man, who wandered toward the bar area in the corner of the room near the French doors that led out to a huge patio and pool area.

While Coop was gazing up at the high ceilings, wondering how much it cost to heat and cool such a place, another server appeared at his side. "Arnold Palmer, sir." He took his, and the server delivered Charlie's to him.

Coop took a sip from the tall glass and caught AB's eye. "The service here is top-notch." He tilted his head toward a table close to the patio that offered a nice view. "Shall we claim a table before we get stuck with some insufferable politician or lobbyist?"

She nodded and took another sip of champagne.

Camille was in her element and beamed. "Victoria knows how to throw a party, trust me. I'm sure dinner will be spectacular."

No sooner had the words left Camille's mouth than Victoria, in a lacy black and gold dress, with Arthur at her side, looking at home in his tux, walked up to her. Camille introduced them to the others, who complimented their gorgeous home.

They were both gracious and relaxed, and Coop could see why Camille liked them. As they were leaving, Victoria patted Coop's arm. "Camille promised me you wouldn't solve the murder too quickly tonight. We want to make it last as long as possible." She winked at him and followed her husband to mingle with other guests.

Coop glanced out the doors to the outdoor space and contemplated sitting by the pool and sipping iced tea all night until the puzzle was solved. He'd been to a couple of these things in the past, and they were always a bit on the juvenile side.

He led the way to the table he wanted and pulled out a chair for AB and then one for Camille. A small gold gift bag was at each place setting, and AB dug into hers, smiling at the high-end rollerball pen, small candle, golf balls, the tiny bag of specialty coffee, and a huge cookie from a posh local bakery.

Coop's eyebrows rose. "I'll trade you my candle for your coffee."

She wagged her finger at him and chuckled.

Content to people watch, Coop settled into his chair as he surveyed the room. He recognized Lois Evans, the Speaker of the House, and Michelle Roberts, the comptroller of Tennessee, among several members of the legislature, including a senator or two. Lots of wealthy Nashvillians from the business community were there, as were many professionals from the legal and medical fields.

It was definitely a mover-and-shaker type of crowd. Exactly the type Coop worked to avoid.

Camille's smile brightened, and she waved when Lois passed close to the table. The older woman with her darted toward their table and Camille. "Francene, it's wonderful to see you," said Camille, who turned to introduce Lois' mother to the others.

Francene bent her head closer to Camille. "Are you saving these seats at your table for someone?"

With a shake of her head, Camille gestured to the four empty chairs. "No, please join us. That would be wonderful."

A look of relief came over Francene. "Thank you. I told Lois I'm not sure I can suffer through another conversation about politics with some of her colleagues."

Coop winked at her. "A woman after my own heart."

She rewarded him with a sweet smile and caught her daughter's eye, who was deep in conversation with Michelle Roberts. She pointed at the chair next to her, and Lois nodded her understanding.

Coop's gaze focused on Michelle, who was hard to miss in her gold gown, with a slit up the side of it to her thigh. Being tall and attractive, she always drew attention, but she had a reputation for being ruthless when it came to her political career. She'd served in the legislature, but she was the current comptroller. Rumor had it her sights were set on the governorship or possibly a seat in Washington, D.C.

Camille studied the other two chairs. "We should try to find two more dinner companions before someone swoops in with the hope of talking Lois' ear off all night." She studied the room, and her smile widened when she spotted a couple by the fireplace. "Coop, be a dear. Go over to invite Maude and Howard to join us."

Coop rose and made his way across the space to the twosome. They lived in Belle Meade and were old friends of Camille's and part of the old-money crowd. They were quiet and polite and, from what Coop knew, needed nothing in the way of information or favors from the political class in Nashville. They'd both inherited their wealth and kept to themselves.

He walked up to them, both holding champagne flutes, and extended his hand to Howard. "Mr. and Mrs. Rutherford. Aunt Camille sent me over to invite you to join our table. We have two empty spots."

Maude was the first to recognize him and smiled. "We'd love to, Cooper. Thank you for coming over to invite us."

Howard nodded. "Yes, we were just wondering where to sit."

Coop gestured across the room. "We're over there." Camille's hand shot up in a wave as soon as he pointed at their table. Coop led the two of them to her, where she greeted them with a warm embrace and encouraged them to take the two seats next to her.

As the guests were gently guided to take their seats, Lois joined them and took the chair next to her mother, who sat next to Coop. Victoria Sinclair climbed the two lowest stairs on the sweeping staircase to the side of their table and picked up a microphone. Her voice filled the room.

"Good evening and welcome to our annual charity gala. I'm Victoria Sinclair, and my husband Arthur and I are so very grateful you've joined us tonight. We're focused on two very worthy charities this year. The first is the local animal rescue we all know and love, and the other is a new charity focused on housing our veterans and connecting them with employment. Just in purchasing your tickets tonight, we're closing in on a quarter million dollars to donate to these two important organizations."

She continued to urge guests to donate via the app they could download, asking them to share it with their employees and colleagues, and called out several large businesses who had pledged huge amounts to help them reach their million-dollar goal.

Coop's interest waned. Instead of listening to her, he focused on watching the faces of those in the room. Many were on their phones, others were gazing out the windows, and a few were fixated on their hostess.

He perked up when she announced dinner would be served and promised to be back with more instructions on the murder mystery part of the evening when dessert arrived.

As soon as the applause for Victoria faded, an army of servers covered the room and delivered serving platters and bowls heaped with pot roast, meat loaf, chicken, brisket, and pulled pork, plus all the sides anyone could want. Coop recognized the fare from Bodine's, a local favorite restaurant with locations across Nashville. They were often voted the best of the city when it came to family food.

His stomach growled as the aroma of the pulled pork and brisket reached his nose. He expected some posh food with tiny portions and swirled colored sauces on his plate. This was a pleasant surprise. Coop eyed the bowl of mashed potatoes the server put near him and leaned closer to AB. "I take back all my complaining about tonight."

She grinned at him. "Not the typical rubber chicken you expected. Camille was right. If *you're* happy, Victoria definitely knows how to throw a party."

"If they bring out their famous strawberry shortcake for

dessert, this will be the best gala ever." Coop chuckled as he heaped some potatoes onto his plate and passed them to AB.

He caught his dad's eye as he was adding gravy to his plate and winked at him. Charlie grinned and nodded while he pointed at his plate. Everyone around the table settled into eating their meal amid quiet conversation centered around the gorgeous chateau and the upcoming outdoor concert season at Silverwood.

Coop didn't have much to add to the discussion and focused on his plate when he wasn't people watching.

Much to Coop's delight, once the servers cleared the dishes from the table, they returned with strawberry shortcake for everyone. As he took his first bite of the sweet berries smothered in sweet whipped cream, Victoria took to her perch.

"I hope you all enjoyed the wonderful meal from Bodine's. I know it's not typical gala cuisine, but I knew I couldn't go wrong with Nashville's favorite eatery." A round of thunderous applause broke out, and she smiled and nodded at the affirmation.

"While you enjoy that to-die-for strawberry shortcake, get ready for the highlight of the evening. We'll be treated to an interactive theatrical performance tonight. Several actors will transport us in time to the 1920's and a fancy gala held in a country house, much like this one. Since our theme is murder, you can guess there will be a victim of a heinous crime."

Amid the murmurs and chuckles, she continued, "Your tablemates are your team, and you'll work together to try to gather clues and solve the murder. For those of you who would rather not participate, you're welcome to stay at your table or wander out by the pool for some fresh air. Once the first act ends, please remove the envelope tucked into the flower arrangement on your table for instructions on where you might find your first clue. All the areas you'll be directed to are on the ground level, so please refrain from going upstairs or using the elevator." She pointed at the velvet rope strung across the stairs behind her.

"Thank you again and enjoy the performance and the rest of the evening. It's been a true pleasure having you with us tonight."

Victoria received more accolades and applause as she made her way from the stairs back to her table, shaking hands along the way.

Coop was savoring his last bite of shortcake when a woman in a red flapper dressed touched his shoulder and smiled as she wandered through the tables to the open area near the fireplace. Several others soon joined her, a mixture of women and men, who kicked off the performance.

Servers poured coffee and tea for guests while they watched the actors engage with each other, trading a few barbs and setting up a host of suspects. Coop ignored AB's side eye when he accepted the offer of coffee and happily stirred sugar into his cup, taking his first sip right before the lights flickered.

As soon as they came on, several of the actresses screamed and pointed to the actor sprawled on the floor with a knife sticking out of his torso. One of the actors reminded everyone to check their envelopes and promised a prize to the first table who returned with the correct killer's name and the motive, which would be found in the clues they were to find.

Maude and Howard, along with Francene, elected to stay at the table and forego traipsing all over the chateau. Lois shrugged. "I'll tag along. I think I have a better chance of escaping more political talk if I'm on the move." She chuckled as she put her napkin on the table.

Chairs slid across the tile floor, and guests rose and milled about, with some heading outside, and others intent on finding clues. Camille stretched her hand to reach for the centerpiece. AB helped her and plucked the envelope from the arrangement.

With a grin, Camille slid the back of it open and read the enclosed card. "It says we need to visit the library and look in the classics for our first clue." She wiggled her brows at Coop. "Ready?"

He couldn't resist the youthful glow of his aunt's excitement. "Ready as ever, Aunt Camille." He pulled out AB's chair, while Charlie did the same for Camille, and together with the Speaker of the House, they set out across the Great Hall in search of the library.

AB leaned close to Coop. "It might be fun, cheer up."

"The only thing I want to find is another piece of that shortcake. Maybe we can detour through the kitchen."

CHAPTER THREE

After Coop insisted they examine the murder victim, who was still in character and playing dead on the floor, Camille led the group past the stairs. After a quick stop in the hallway for the ladies room, she pointed further down to a set of French doors. "Here we are."

Camille turned the handle, and they followed her into the mahogany-paneled room, lit only by the soft lamps on the large desk near the window with a view of the edge of the patio and the grass of the backyard.

The walls were lined with dark-wood bookcases, filled with hundreds of volumes of books. Coop's feet sank into a thick area rug covering the wooden flooring. He inhaled the spicy aroma of men's aftershave mixed with the scent of paper and a hint of vanilla that always seems to be present in libraries. He'd read it had something to do with an ingredient in paper that was closely related to the popular spice. Whatever it was, he'd always found it inviting and comforting.

As he contemplated the shelves, Charlie and Camille

stepped further into the room. Moments later, he heard Camille gasp. "Oh, my. I think they've led us to a surprise second victim."

Coop frowned and hurried to a sitting area where a velvet settee was nestled between two leather chairs. In one of the chairs, the body of a woman was sprawled, as if she'd slid from a seated position. Her heels were caught in the bottom of her gown. Coop recognized the gold glow of the fabric even before AB used the hem of her dress to turn on the touch-activated lamp next to the settee.

As soon as the light shone across the woman, Lois gasped. "That's Michelle."

Charlie glanced at his son. "Do you think she's part of the act?"

Coop pointed at the champagne flute on the floor at the side of the chair. "I don't think so." He took a step closer to her and put his fingers on her neck to feel for a pulse.

After several seconds, he moved this fingers and waited again, then shook his head. "She's dead."

Coop's hand went to his pocket, where he always kept a pair of gloves. Not in his tuxedo pants, though. Had he been wearing his usual jeans and t-shirt, he would have had them. Coop ushered the others away from the body and asked Camille and Charlie to find Victoria and Arthur. "Don't touch that door handle though. Use your sleeve or a napkin or something only on the very tip. We don't want to mess up any chance for fingerprints if they're needed." Lois followed them and waited inside the door. Coop pulled out his cell phone and tapped Ben's name.

Ben's cheerful voice, compensating for the loud

background noise, blared in his ear. "Did you ditch the party, and on your way to sit with us?"

"Afraid not. I'm also going to ruin your evening. We've found a dead body at the gala. It's Michelle Roberts, Tennessee's comptroller."

"You are joking, right?"

"No, I'm not. It's going to turn into a circus quickly. I was hoping you could get here without drawing any unnecessary attention."

"I'll be there as soon as I can, and I'll roll Kate too. Expect the paramedics first. Keep everyone out of the scene for me, will ya? This is going to be a shitshow. Do you think it's a homicide?"

"Hard to say. No apparent indicators at the scene. Glass of champagne near her, so poison is a possibility, but the docs will have to tell us. Sorry, Ben. I'll do my best until your guys get here." He disconnected and caught AB's eyes. "See anything?"

She shook her head. "Like you said, just the champagne glass. It's got a piece missing that's next to it there, in the rug."

Coop nodded and leaned forward, checking the leather chair. "Looks like a cell phone wedged in the cushion next to her, but we'll leave that for Ben's crew."

AB darted her eyes toward the door where Lois stood. She lowered her voice. "Do you think it's natural causes?"

He shrugged. "I don't know. Could be. I don't see any blood or marks on her neck. Nothing on her arms or hands to indicate any defensive maneuvers. It's hard to say until they examine her." He pointed to the window. "That's the only other access point."

AB nodded. "It's locked. I checked while you were on the phone. Didn't touch anything though."

"We need to keep everyone here and keep them calm, so Ben and his team can do their jobs."

Coop slipped the notebook he always carried from his inside jacket pocket and walked toward Lois. Her pale face and wide eyes gave him pause. "Are you okay? Do you need to sit down? Maybe have a glass of water?"

She shook her head. "I'm fine, just shocked. I was just talking to her before I sat down with all of you."

"Do you know who she sat with tonight?"

Her forehead creased. "I saw Maxine with her. She's her personal assistant. Diane Thornfield was here. I assume she was with Michelle. She's been her campaign manager throughout her career. I noticed Michelle's husband Joe, uh, Ward is his last name, I think. I saw him come through the door late, just as we were finishing dessert."

Coop scribbled in his notebook. "What did you and Michelle discuss?"

Lois sighed. "Michelle is very focused on corruption and while I know she is sincere about her quest to root it out, the temperature within the constituency right now is one that is hungry for accountability from politicians. She knew it would play well in her bid for her next office. She wanted me to know she was planning to shine a light on the party. Our party. She hinted that some very big players could go down."

Coop's brows rose as she talked.

Victoria and Arthur approached the door, worry etched on their faces. Coop and AB followed Lois out the door, where they stood in front of it. Mr. Sinclair looked at Coop and whispered. "Camille said there's a body in the library?"

Coop lowered his voice. "I'm afraid so. Initially, Camille thought it was part of the game, but clearly, the woman is dead. It's Michelle Roberts. I've called the police, and they're on the way. The paramedics should be here soon. Maybe you can direct them to the patio entrance so they draw the least attention?"

He nodded. "I'll get out there right now."

"Does her husband know? He was sitting next to her." Victoria's voice trembled as she murmured the name to Coop.

Coop shook his head as he added Joe Ward to the names in his notebook. "We need to wait for the detectives."

AB reached out for Victoria's arm. "Do you think you could make an announcement and get everyone back to their tables right now? You can just say you have an important update and by the time they're all seated, hopefully, the police will be here and can take it from there. If you need to say something, just say you've called the paramedics for a guest and want to keep everyone out of the way and calm. The detectives won't want anyone leaving until they examine the scene."

Worry filled her eyes. Coop put a hand on her shoulder. "You'll be fine. You're a natural. Give everyone more dessert and drinks, and they'll be like putty in your hands."

A weak smile lifted the corners of her mouth as she nodded. "I'll do my best."

Coop stepped closer to his dad. "You and Camille take Lois back to the table. She's shook up. AB and I will stay here and make sure nobody enters the library."

Charlie nodded and offered Lois his arm. "Shall we go back to the table and join the others?"

She accepted his arm, Camille took the other, and the three of them set out for the table, while Mrs. Sinclair made for the stairs and the microphone. Coop scanned the hallway that connected the library to the Great Hall and noticed there were several other rooms along it before it fed back to the Great Hall.

As Victoria asked everyone to return to their tables, Coop saw two paramedics come through the patio doors with their gear. As Mr. Sinclair led them to the library, several heads turned.

Right on cue, Victoria noticed and let her visitors know that they'd called the paramedics for a guest and asked that everyone remain at their tables and await further information. She added that the servers would be coming around to take drink orders and offered seconds on desserts for everyone.

While she was talking, Coop let the paramedics know he had checked for a pulse but didn't find one. They did the same and after listening with his stethoscope, the lead paramedic shook his head. "She's gone." He looked up at Coop. "Did she complain about not feeling well?"

Coop shook his head. "We found her like this. I've called the police, and they're enroute."

He took hold of his bag and stood with his partner, away from the body toward the entrance. "We'll wait here for them."

"Just don't touch the door handles; we're not sure what we're dealing with here." Coop felt responsible for the scene, and stood with them, not wanting to leave anything to chance. Moments later, Kate and Ben appeared at the door.

Coop took the pocket square he'd been using and eased the door open. "I've never been happier to see the two of you."

Kate, dressed in her typical matching pants and jacket, followed Ben, who was wearing jeans and a t-shirt, with a Nashville Police jacket over it. Coop gave them a rundown of what they'd found when they arrived at the library. "I checked her pulse, and then we all moved away from the body. Nobody has touched the interior handle of the door.

We used fabric on the very end to open it to try to minimize disturbing any prints you might need. Camille opened it with the exterior handle when we arrived before we knew."

Kate interviewed the paramedics, while Ben focused on the body, asking Coop questions while he surveyed it and the entire scene. After a quick conversation, Kate jotted some information in her notebook and dismissed the two paramedics.

Ben tilted his head when Coop pointed out the cell phone. "Techs should be here soon, and we can get some photos and get the doctor in here to take a look at her before we move her. Like you said, no visible signs of a struggle, save for the glass of champagne."

Coop nodded. "Which could have fallen if she had a heart attack or whatever."

"Right." Ben sighed. "I hate to think of keeping all these people here any longer than necessary, but if this turns out to be a crime, we're going to have to talk to them."

Kate gestured toward the entrance. "I'll get a guest list and get a team in here to collect contact information from everyone."

Ben sighed. "Let's hold everyone at Ms. Roberts' table, along with anyone we can connect to her, and we'll interview them more extensively. I'll go talk to the husband. I just need to find a private room away from the crowd. Everyone else, let's just release them once we have their information."

Kate nodded. "On it, boss. I'll get all the catering staff as well and hold anyone who came in contact with her. I'll see if we can figure out where she obtained the champagne."

Ben glanced over at Coop. "Jimmy is out of town, so it's just the two of us tonight. Can you and AB pitch in and help collect names until reinforcements arrive? The sooner we can get rid of some of these folks, the better."

Coop nodded. "Sure, we can do that. Are you okay getting a statement from my dad and Camille tomorrow?"

Ben nodded. "Sure, you can send them home for now."

Two uniformed officers arrived, and Ben asked them to secure the scene and keep everyone away from the library. Ben tilted his head at Kate. "Give the guests the news and if Coop and AB run across anyone who had contact with the deceased tonight, they'll hold them for you."

"On it." She left the room, and Coop and AB followed her, while Ben went to find Michelle's husband and deliver the sad news.

As soon as Ben escorted the stocky man from his wife's table, Kate picked up Victoria's microphone and explained a guest had died. While she was waiting for the gasps, whispered questions, and sobs to subside, the evidence technicians arrived and descended upon the library. Kate asked everyone to remain in their seats until their information had been collected and promised they would work as quickly as possible to release everyone.

Kate whispered to Coop to make sure to separate any guests who had contact with Ms. Roberts, to keep them from talking to each other, and set out for Michelle's table. Coop stopped in the kitchen and asked the catering manager if they had a layout of the tables for serving purposes. She gave him two copies of the layout with table numbers. He took a photo of it with his phone and sent it to Kate and Ben, since it would be useful for identification of the seating positions relative to the victim.

He gave the spare copy to AB, and they split the room and set out on their quest to collect contact information from each table.

Coop tackled his table first and filled in the contact information from Maude and Howard, along with Speaker

Evans and her mother. He asked Speaker Evans to wait for the police and not talk to anyone, since she'd been in contact with Ms. Roberts earlier in the evening.

He slipped the keys to Camille's car to his dad. "Ben said you and Aunt Camille can head home, and he'll get a statement from you both tomorrow, since you were in the room when we discovered the body."

Camille overheard him and pointed at Francene. "We can drop Francene at home too. She doesn't need to wait all night for Lois to be released." They collected their gift bags and made for the door.

Coop made a note on the sheet Kate had provided for witness contact information. With Lois remaining, Coop moved to the next table.

As the guests were cleared out and more help arrived from Ben's team, things moved quickly. Ben and Kate were using the study and the music room to conduct individual interviews. When AB and Coop finished their lists, they found an empty table and waited.

A few of the catering staff were still on the premises and came by with trays of iced tea, coffee, and water for the remaining guests. Coop joined AB in selecting a tall iced tea and a glass of water. He gulped down the water in one long swallow. "Wow, I needed that. Too much talking in the last hour."

AB finished her water and nodded. "Yeah, not the evening I expected."

They each had their list of witnesses and while Coop had already recorded those who were connected to Ms. Roberts from his sheet, he scanned AB's and added the names from her list to his notebook.

He finished and returned it to his jacket pocket. He

lowered his voice. "Interesting that Michelle's ex-husband and their daughter were here tonight."

AB nodded. "I got the feeling there was no love lost between them. Barry Marshall is his name, and the daughter is Bridget. Michelle kept her maiden name. Ben scooped both of them away as soon as he found out they were here."

"From what I gathered from Lois Evans, Michelle was set on winning a seat in D.C., specifically the seat held by Marcus Ryle, who was also here tonight." Coop's brows rose. "Way too many politicians in one place, if you ask me."

AB grinned. "Oh, and Emily Harper. Don't forget her. She's already announced that she's running for Ryle's seat. She's a popular state senator already, so she's considered a strong rival."

Coop lowered his voice. "Don't I always say nothing good comes when too many politicians and rich people are gathered?" He sighed. "Tonight is a prime example."

CHAPTER FOUR

S unday morning, Coop woke up exhausted, having not slept much after a late night at the Sinclair estate waiting on Ben. It was after midnight by the time he officially interviewed them and gave Coop and AB a ride home.

Ben promised to stop by to collect statements from Charlie and Camille and left them at the door with a weak smile on his tired face. Coop offered AB one of the guestrooms, but she opted to drive home in the wee hours of the morning.

Coop yawned and looked over at the chair where Gus often slept when he wasn't in his dog bed. The chair was empty. No doubt Gus was having breakfast and getting spoiled by Aunt Camille.

After a long shower, Coop emerged, ready for coffee and something to eat. He wandered into the kitchen and found Charlie, Camille, and AB all gathered at the island countertop. Warm cinnamon rolls dripping with cream cheese frosting sat on a platter in front of them, and Coop breathed in the scent of fresh coffee.

"Morning, all," he said, reaching for a cup from the cabinet. "When did you get here, AB?"

"Just a few minutes ago. Camille called and said she made cinnamon rolls." Gus was snuggled up to AB, as close as he could get without climbing into her lap.

Coop took his first sip and closed his eyes, letting the rich liquid work its magic. As he took a seat and reached for a cinnamon roll, the doorbell rang.

Charlie gestured toward the entryway. "I'll get it." Gus followed him just in case he needed backup.

Moments later, they returned with Ben, who looked as tired as he had when he left them last night.

Camille poured him a cup of coffee and suggested they all gather in the dining room, where it would be more comfortable. Charlie carried the cinnamon rolls, and AB grabbed a plate for Ben.

After Camille made sure Ben had a cinnamon roll, everyone dug into the gooey goodness. Ben groaned as he took his first bite. "That hits the spot. Thanks, Camille."

She blushed as she reached for her cup of tea. "You poor dear, I'm sure you've been up half the night."

Ben nodded as he cut off another bite. "It's been a long and eventful night with my phone ringing constantly. In fact, as soon as I can collect your statements, I'm due at the medical examiner's. I'm hoping he has some answers for me."

Camille tsked as she shook her head. "It's horrible that Ms. Roberts died and at such a lovely event. Victoria was so distraught last night. The whole thing is very upsetting."

As they finished their breakfast treats, Ben asked if he could chat with Charlie, and Coop followed them into the sitting room, where Charlie explained what he witnessed and wrote out a brief statement.

"I've got very little to add and nothing of any consequence, I'm sure," said Charlie, handing Ben the paper.

"Thanks for this," said Ben. "It's a matter of making sure we capture everything from those who were present when Ms. Roberts was discovered."

Charlie nodded and glanced over at Gus, who was lounging by the doorway. "I think I'll take Gus out for a short walk around the neighborhood."

The dog's ears lifted, and he stood, wagging his tail, ready for whatever adventure Charlie had in mind.

Coop grinned. "Looks like he's ready. Just make sure you take your phone and don't let him rush you."

Charlie patted Gus on the head. "He's a good boy and adjusts to my slower pace. We'll be back in an hour or so."

Coop retrieved Gus' leash on their way back to the dining room and stood in the doorway, watching his two favorite guys set out down the street before he rejoined the others in the dining room.

When Camille finished signing her statement, Ben took it and slipped it into the folder he had in his leather portfolio. "With you being in some of the same circles as the guests from last night, what do you know about Michelle and the people in her orbit?"

Aunt Camille's penciled-on eyebrows arched. "I don't know her personally. I do know of her ex-husband Barry. He's been in real estate forever. Old family firm. His first wife died. When he and Michelle married, she joined him to work there. I'm not sure if she was in real estate and if that's how they met. He's quite a bit older than Michelle. They've been divorced, oh, I would guess close to ten years."

Ben nodded as he added a note to his file. After a sip of

tea, Camille added, "Most everyone thought it strange that the daughter stayed with Barry when they divorced. Michelle doesn't strike me as the maternal type, so maybe that's why."

Ben tapped his pen on the cover of his portfolio. "Any scuttlebutt about the reason they divorced? Any affairs or anything like that?"

Camille's lips flattened. "Well, at the time, it was rumored that Michelle was stepping out on Barry. Maybe the age difference was too much. I know after they divorced, she dated several men. There was some gossip at the time, but I wasn't all that dialed into her crowd. She's much younger, and I don't think her family is from here."

After finishing the last of his coffee, Ben returned the pen to his pocket. "Well, I better get going. Thanks for your help and the delicious cinnamon roll." He glanced over at Coop. "I'll see you Friday, if not before."

"I'll walk you out," offered Coop.

Ben said his goodbyes and wandered outside. He stopped at the door to his car. "If you think of anything else you noticed last night, let me know."

Coop frowned. "I get the feeling you're not convinced it was natural causes?"

Ben shook his head. "Doc found a fresh needle mark on her hip area. Nothing on the preliminary tox screen, but he's running some special tests, so I'm hoping we have a firm answer today. It's definitely suspicious at best."

"Oh, boy. From what AB and I gleaned last night, Michelle was, how do I say it tactfully? Ruthless. Ambitious. I think someone even said she had killer instincts when it came to politics and sounds like she was a threat to her own party."

With a heavy sigh, Ben nodded. "Yeah, if it was murder,

the suspect list won't be short." He climbed behind the wheel. "Thanks again for helping last night and keeping the scene secure until we could get there."

"No problem. If we think of anything, I'll give you a shout." As Ben left the driveway, Coop hurried back to the house to pour himself another cup of coffee.

He brought it to the table, shrugged off the disapproving look from AB, and proceeded to savor another sip. They were still at the table when Gus and Charlie came through the door.

Gus rushed to Coop's side and then hurried around the table to greet Camille and AB. Coop glanced across the table and caught AB's eye. "We've got tickets to the Dogs & Dogwood Festival at Silverwood today. You're welcome to join us."

"Aww, that sounds fun, but I need to get home and clean my house, do some laundry, all that stuff I didn't do yesterday because I was busy getting ready for the gala."

Camille shook her head. "You looked absolutely stunning, AB. We'll have to go to another event soon so you can wear that dress again. Last night was definitely a bust."

With a slow grin, Coop chuckled. "Dead bodies do tend to put a damper on things."

Camille collected the plates and silverware. "I do feel bad for Victoria. She worked so hard on the gala."

Coop stood and helped gather the cups. "The food was excellent and as far as galas go, it's near the top of my list. Notwithstanding the dead body, of course. Victoria will be known as the killer hostess. Just think they could have a new slogan. Sinclair Chateau: the place for killer parties."

AB rolled her eyes at Coop.

With her head shaking and her arms full of dishes, Camille led the way to the kitchen. As Coop set the cups in the sink, he snickered when his aunt let a chuckle escape. He put a hand on her shoulder. "Don't tell Victoria I said that. I'm just joking."

She smiled. "Oh, don't worry. I would never tell her as long as you promise not to tell her I laughed. Being married to your uncle all those years, I came to appreciate and even share his sometimes inappropriate sense of humor in the face of such ghastly circumstances. It was a way of coping with all the nastiness he saw, so I understand why you joke."

She started rinsing the dishes. "Hopefully, when the news wears off, she'll feel better. Of course, she feels horrible for Michelle and her family, but she's worried the whole thing will tarnish the Sinclair name and the fundraising for the two charities. I told her I'd help make a few calls to encourage people to donate, since the evening was cut short."

AB came through the door with Charlie. "Thanks for breakfast. I'll see you at the office in the morning, Coop."

Camille wiped her hands on her apron and turned away from the sink. "Are you sure we can't persuade you to join us at Silverwood? It's lovely this time of year, and I've got plenty of tickets with my membership."

She glanced down at Gus, who was leaning against her, his eyes pleading. AB sighed. "Let me run home and start a load of laundry. I'll come for a bit but can't stay long."

Camille clapped her hands together. "Wonderful. They've got a whole slew of food trucks and vendors there, so I'm not making my usual Sunday supper tonight. We're going to splurge and eat there. We've got a table in the Platinum Donor Tent, and you're welcome to stay and have dinner with us."

"What time are you going?" AB asked, taking her keys from her pocket.

"Probably around two o'clock, but don't rush. Whenever

you get there is fine. They're open until six o'clock for the festival. You can get your chores done and then come and relax."

Coop bent down and petted Gus' head. "Just text me when you get there, and we'll keep an eye out for you. Dad and I are looking forward to the beer garden."

AB laughed and stepped toward the door. "Sounds good. I'll text you and see you in a couple of hours."

———

After Gus, Aunt Camille, and his dad took a nap, Coop drove them all to Silverwood. The gorgeous botanical garden and mansion served as an art museum sat amid over fifty acres of land not far from Aunt Camille's estate. Their year-round events were popular with locals and tourists alike. From the looks of the parking lot, there were several people with the same idea on a gorgeous and sunny Sunday afternoon.

Camille led the way to the ticket booth, where her old friend Eula Mae was working. After a short visit with her, the three of them walked by the visitor center with Gus' nose high in the air, sniffing at all the food trucks parked in the lot nearest the entrance.

Coop surveyed the offerings, his future plans focused on the burger truck, but also interested in the enchilada one. They wandered the pathways through the colorful blooms of tulips, with Gus sniffing every flower and bush. As they neared the mansion, Camille pointed at the white tent on the Great Lawn. "That's ours."

They walked past another paved lot, filled with more vendors and food. Charlie spotted the Music City Creamery truck. "Oh, we'll have to get ice cream before too long."

Camille pointed at the dog bandana booth and the pet

artist, who was doing sketches of dogs while the owners waited. "I think Gus would look dashing in a bandana."

Gus looked up at Coop. His eyes were begging for help. Coop chuckled as Camille darted to the booth. Minutes later, she returned with a bag full of bandanas. She tugged one out, a bright green one with paw prints on it. Gus endured the installation of it around his neck.

His love for Camille was such that he tolerated her sometimes whimsical nonsense, although his eyes held a look of exasperation. Camille stepped back to admire him and adjusted it so it hung down his chest. "Oh, you look so handsome, Gus. It's perfect and so bright and cheerful. Like you."

Gus' tongue swept across her hand. All was forgiven.

Camille backtracked to their tent. Charlie and Coop, holding onto Gus' leash, followed her to the entrance. She found their table, sporting a little sign with her name. A beverage station was set up alongside the tent, with soft drinks, water, tea, and lemonade.

Camille pointed at the copper bucket filled with ice. "I'm going to stick to soft drinks, but you two enjoy the beer garden. I can drive us home."

Charlie grinned, and he took hold of Gus' leash. "Come on, buddy. Let's sniff out some beer, and then we'll grab some ice cream."

Coop's phone chimed. And he read a text from AB letting him know she was at the entrance. He typed in a quick reply directing her to the beer garden. It was situated not far from the building where the garden's café and gift shop were housed.

Charlie found seats for the three of them at the end of one of the long tables, and Gus relaxed at his feet, while Coop went to fetch their beers. Moments later, Gus' tail whipped back and forth on the grass. He spotted AB before she saw Charlie.

Coop returned with two plastic cups of beer and set them on the table at the same time AB arrived. Coop glanced down at the beer. "I figured you wouldn't want one, but if you do, feel free, and I'll get one more."

She shook her head. "Nah, I think I'll pass on that."

Charlie took a sip from his cup. "How about some ice cream? They've got a truck here."

"That sounds better."

Charlie dug out his wallet. "I'll buy if you fly." He pointed toward the lot where the food trucks and vendors were staged.

AB took the twenty-dollar bill he offered. "Deal. What flavor would you like?"

Charlie grinned and said, "Surprise us. Whatever you think."

Coop took a seat across from his dad and was just about to take his first sip when his phone rang. He frowned when he saw it was from Aunt Camille. He tapped the green button.

"Coop, I just got a call from Victoria Sinclair. She's in a state, and she and Arthur need to see you right away. She apologized for disturbing us on a Sunday but said she couldn't wait until your office opened tomorrow. I told her you'd be over as soon as you could."

As he disconnected, AB arrived with three bowls of ice cream and set them on the table. "I took Camille some pralines and cream." She glanced at Coop and frowned. "What's wrong?"

"Aunt Camille just called and said Victoria and Arthur want to see me right away."

Charlie took a bowl of the strawberry. "Surely, they can wait until you finish your ice cream."

AB handed Coop a bowl of mocha chip, while she took the chocolate. "I agree, let's finish our treat, and then I'll drive us over to see what they want."

Coop shrugged and slid the first bite of the chocolate and coffee flavor he loved into his mouth. As he went back for another spoonful, his cell phone rang. He dug it from his pocket. "It's Ben."

As he answered, he stepped away from the table and the other patrons of the beer garden. He found refuge under a tree. "Sorry, Ben, I couldn't hear you."

"I just wanted you to know, the Michelle Roberts case has been declared a homicide. The medical examiner was suspicious about a few things and especially that fresh needle mark on her hip, so he ran some specific tests and found succinylcholine in her system."

"Wow, that definitely eliminates natural causes. I just got summoned to the Sinclair estate. Aunt Camille said it was urgent."

"Hmm, interesting. Our public information team is working on a press release as we speak. I asked them to hold off releasing it until tomorrow afternoon to try to buy us a little time. With something this high profile, it's hard to keep things quiet."

"This one has all the makings of a media feeding frenzy. Not to mention a huge list of potential suspects. Sorry, Ben, I know how much you hate cases like this one."

"Yeah, you and me both. I gotta run. Talk to you later."

Coop disconnected, finished off his ice cream, and walked back to the beer garden. Coop slid his untouched beer down the table and offered it to one of the guys sitting

35

two chairs away from him. "I have to leave; you're welcome to it."

"Thanks, man," said the man, who was finishing his own beer. "Appreciate it."

Coop took hold of Gus' leash. "AB and I are heading over to the Sinclair estate. Are you okay to look after Gus and get home with Camille?"

"Sure thing, Coop. Gus and I will be fine. I'm sorry your outing was cut short. Maybe you'll be able to come back. I know Camille planned to stay until they close and have dinner here."

Coop had a feeling they'd be working through dinner. "I suspect we'll be at the office working."

Charlie's smile faded. "I'm so sorry, but we'll be fine. Don't worry about us." He finished the last swallow of beer and tossed his cup in the garbage.

Coop nodded. "I'll call you later."

AB patted Gus on the head. "Thanks for the ice cream treat, Charlie."

"Anytime, AB. Try not to work too hard, you two." He took the leash and led Gus toward Camille's tent.

As he and AB hurried to the parking lot, Coop lowered his voice. "Ben called to let us know Michelle Roberts was murdered."

AB's eyes widened. "This day just got a lot more interesting."

CHAPTER FIVE

It didn't take long for them to make the drive to the Sinclair estate, where the security gates were closed. AB hit the button on the intercom with the camera, and the gate swung open. She drove her VW Beetle up the sweeping driveway and parked in front of the door.

By the time they climbed the steps, Victoria had the door open and, with a forced smile, welcomed them inside. "Thank you so much for coming. I apologize for ruining your Sunday. Arthur and I are in the study. Can I offer you something to drink?"

Coop shook his head. "No, thank you. We're fine."

He and AB followed her down the hallway, past the library, to a large room outfitted with two desks, plenty of chairs, and a large television mounted on the wall. The windows provided a view of the pool area, and Coop noticed the French doors that led out to the patio.

Arthur rose from the chair behind his desk and joined them at the sitting area, outfitted with leather chairs and a velvet settee that matched the one in the library. Coop noted the tired look in their eyes and the slump of their shoulders.

Arthur waited for Coop and AB to take their seats before sitting next to his wife on the settee. "We've just heard the police have ruled Ms. Roberts' death a homicide. While we have the utmost respect for the police and their abilities, we want to get out in front of this and wish to hire you to find the culprit."

Victoria took a deep breath. "It was upsetting enough to have Michelle die at the gala, but a murder, right here in our house." She shook her head. "We're already being mentioned as the place where Michelle Roberts died. Now, we'll be known as the house where she was murdered. We just want to restore our good name, and the quicker the killer is found the better."

Arthur patted his wife's arm. "We hate to think we allowed a murderer in our home and are sickened that the charities we support have been sullied by all of this." He pointed at a file on his desk. "I've got the guest list with contact information, the valet list of vehicles, plus all the security footage from our cameras that night. Only exterior cameras; we don't have interior coverage. We've provided the same to the police."

As her husband spoke, Coop noticed a very slight shake of Victoria's head. He surmised she had a tremor that he hadn't noticed the night of the gala. Most likely exacerbated by stress.

"Money is no object," said Arthur. "We trust you and hope you'll take the case."

At those words, Coop's focus shifted to her husband. Arthur removed a check from his jacket pocket and handed it to Coop. "Here's a retainer to get you started."

Coop glanced and forced himself not to whistle at the

generous amount. As much as he hated high-profile cases and the thought of dealing with the political and wealthy crowd on the suspect list, the agency could use the money and even more, Aunt Camille would never forgive him if he turned down her friends. "Sure, we'll take it."

Victoria let out a long sigh and with tears in her eyes, she reached out for Coop's hand. "Thank you, Cooper. I knew we could count on you."

"Just so you know, there's a good chance the police will solve this one quickly. This may not even be necessary."

Arthur nodded. "We hope so, but we want someone who is working for us and focused only on this case. The police have more than this to deal with and with a small firm like yours, we know this case will be your priority."

Coop rose and pointed at the French doors. "I noticed the library had no exterior entrance point, but this room does. Do any other rooms on the first floor have similar access from the outside? Do you remember if all the doors were locked the night of the gala?"

Arthur nodded. "Yes, we made a conscious decision to keep all the doors locked, except for the doors off the Great Hall out to the pool and patio and of course, the front entrance. Not to say someone couldn't have unlocked a door like this one, but we have cameras covering all the access points. I've reviewed them myself and saw nothing untoward as far as entry from the outside."

Coop nodded. "Okay, we'll take what you have and get started on it. If we run into any questions, we'll be in touch."

Arthur pulled the thick file folder from the corner of his desk and pointed at the business card clipped to it. "I've added my cell and Victoria's on the back. Call us day or night with anything you need."

"One other thing," said Coop. "We have a good working

relationship with the Nashville Police and have worked closely with them in the past, even consulting at times. I will be letting Ben Mason know we've been retained to investigate."

Arthur nodded. "We understand and have no objection to you using our name as your client. It may open doors for you when it comes to chatting with the guests on the list. Let them know they're free to contact us if they have any doubts."

AB shook both their hands and pulled a business card from her purse. "Here's our contact information, although you can always get in touch via Camille." She smiled and followed Coop to the door.

"We'll be in touch when we learn anything," said Coop, as they walked outside toward AB's car.

As he folded his long legs into the small space, he handed AB the hefty file to hold. "I think we're going to need a bigger whiteboard for all these suspects."

———

AB drove straight to the office, where she started a pot of decaf brewing, while Coop laid out the contents of the file folder on the conference table. He added a container of colored highlighters and pens to their work area.

As he was perusing the guest list, his phone rang. He smiled when he saw his dad's photo.

"Hey, Dad. Everything okay?"

"We're fine. Are you at the office?"

"Yes, we just got here."

"We finished up dinner and brought you and AB some takeout from the food trucks. Camille says we're your personal Uber Grubbers or whatever they call it."

Coop laughed. "Oh, you guys are the best. You can leave Gus here with us, too. I'm sure he's tired from all the activity at Silverwood."

"He's definitely ready for a nap." He chuckled. "As are the two of us. We'll be there in a few minutes."

"I'll meet you at the back door."

He made his way into the main part of the office where AB was at her desk, collecting her notepad. "Coffee's almost done."

"Dad just called, and they're dropping off Gus and dinner for us."

"Oh, even better. I was looking forward to checking out those food trucks."

Coop hurried to the kitchen and added Gus' food to his bowl. He was bound to be hungry after an afternoon of exercise. As soon as he filled his bowl with fresh water and added his dinner bowl to the mat, the flash in the window prompted Coop to catch Camille's sedan as it pulled into the back parking lot. He made his way outside. "Thanks for watching my boy and for dinner."

He took the bag of food from his dad, and Gus leapt from the backseat. "Don't work too late, Coop," said Camille.

"We'll try not to. The police have ruled Michelle Roberts' death a homicide. This case is a doozy, and Arthur and Victoria hired us to try to figure it out."

Camille's hand went to her throat. "Oh, dear. That's not good news. No wonder Victoria sounded so upset. Try to get home at a decent hour. You'll have a long week ahead of you and need some rest."

Coop nodded and watched them drive away while Gus followed him to the back door.

As soon as they were inside, Gus made a beeline for his bowl and proceeded to gulp down his dinner. Minutes later, he finished, slurped up some water, and hurried to find AB.

Coop set the takeout bag on the kitchen table. He unpacked it and discovered burgers, fries, and enchiladas. His stomach growled, and his heart warmed with the realization of how lucky he was to have Camille and his dad.

AB came through the door with her furry shadow. "Ooh, that looks delicious."

"Help yourself. They brought us enough to have lunch tomorrow too."

After some nonproductive begging, Gus wandered away, and the click of his toenails on the floor let them know he was in Coop's office, no doubt ready for a nap in his chair.

As they noshed on the juicy burgers stuffed with cheddar cheese, opting to save the enchiladas for tomorrow, they reviewed the guest list and batted around suspects and possible motives. Coop reached for another napkin. "We have to check out the ex-husband and the current husband."

AB nodded. "Right and if we can eliminate them, they might have some insights into others who might have a motive."

Coop plucked another parmesan-crusted fry from the pile. "I also want to go to Michelle's office and talk to the people who work there. Maybe there's been some recent kerfuffle with someone or a constituent or an associate on the guest list."

"Camille mentioned there was gossip about her having an affair before. Maybe she's having one now?" AB's brows rose.

"Always a chance." He pointed at the drawing of Michelle's table at the gala. "Her personal assistant, Maxine Solano, would probably know something about that." He took his last bite of his burger. "Can you research succinylcholine and find out where one might obtain it and how it works? I'll see if I can get us some time with Maxine, Barry the ex, and the current hubby."

AB closed the lid on her takeout container. "On it."

"Then, we'll have to figure out how to tackle the political animals. Maybe Lois Evans can help pave the way. I'll need to give it some thought."

———

Victoria's list, complete with cell phone numbers, proved to be helpful, as did the fact that Coop was working for her and Arthur. Barry Marshall expressed his admiration for the Sinclairs and was willing to meet Coop and AB tonight, citing a busy day tomorrow. He invited them to his house, which was only minutes away in Forest Hills.

When Coop shared the news with AB, she gave him the once over, and her disapproving look settled on his worn shirt emblazoned with IT WAS ME. I LET THE DOGS OUT.

He glanced down at the shirt he'd chosen for the dog festival at Silverwood and made his way over to the armoire in his office where clean polo shirts hung. He grabbed a blue one with the Harrington & Associations logo and changed into it. He was still underdressed for the swanky neighborhood but hoped with it being the weekend, Mr. Marshall would understand.

Coop managed to get Gus in the backseat of AB's Beetle, and he bundled himself and the thick case file into the passenger compartment. He asked AB to drop him home so he could pick up his Jeep and leave Gus to rest with Camille and Charlie.

With Gus settled, AB followed Coop the few miles to the Marshall property. A tall security gate stopped them from entering the long driveway, but when Coop announced them both, the gate opened.

The driveway wound through trees until it revealed a beautiful brick Georgian-style mansion set among the foliage. A tall man with silvery gray hair met them at the door, and they stepped into the immaculate and quiet home.

After introducing himself and shaking their hands, Barry pointed down the entry hall. "We can sit in the living room." He led the way and asked if they wanted something to drink before taking a seat in a high-backed leather chair.

Coop met his striking blue eyes. "Thanks again for seeing us on such short notice. We appreciate it. We're very sorry for your loss. As I explained, we're looking into your ex-wife's death at the Sinclair estate. Did you interact with Michelle that night?"

He shook his head. "No. We often found ourselves at the same type of events but haven't met or spoken one-on-one for several years. Well, since Bridget was much younger, and we were coordinating things for her. Our divorce wasn't exactly amicable, but over time, we've managed to tolerate each other when we find ourselves in the same place."

Coop nodded. "We know Bridget was there, and your older sons from your prior marriage were also with you. We'd like to speak to all of them too."

With a nod, Barry added, "Bridget is staying at my sister's right now. They're quite close. Have been ever since the divorce. Penelope took on the role that Michelle vacated with Bridget." He shook his head. "If not for Poppy, I'm not sure what I would have done. Teenage girls are tough enough, without adding a messy divorce. Michelle was very focused on her career and less so on Bridget."

He took his cell phone from the side table. "I can give you phone numbers for Baron and Adam. We all live here on the estate, in separate homes. My first wife passed away after a lengthy illness, and the boys and I are very close. It's wonderful having them here on the property. If you follow the main drive you came in on as it continues past this house, you'll find the others, including Poppy. Her place is the next one you'll see. I can call her and see if she and Bridget are up for a visit. Bridget has been quite emotional since her mother's death."

As soon as he finished reciting their contact information, AB sighed. "That's understandable. Losing your mom is never easy. From how you phrased it earlier, I assumed she and Michelle weren't close?"

He shook his head. "They weren't. The divorce was tough. Over time, it's gotten better, but Bridget never forgave Michelle, and her mother was absent from much of her life. Michelle and her husband own a chain of wellness spas. You know the kind with yoga and a gym, plus all the treatments, cosmetic fillers, you name it. She made sure Bridget had a membership, and she sent gifts and money. In the last couple of years, she made more of an effort, but they weren't what you'd call close. Bridget's at Vanderbilt now. Took a couple years off after high school and spent a year traveling Europe. She's twenty-three but behind. She'll be a junior this fall. I think she's finally settling in and finding her pathway."

Coop finished adding a note in his notebook. "Can you think of anyone who might want to harm Michelle or know of anyone threatening her?"

Barry chuckled. "Michelle is abrasive at best. She's made her share of what you might call enemies, but I don't have any personal knowledge of anyone who'd want to harm her. Her political ambitions are well known, and she's never been afraid of ruffling feathers. Her latest is the announcement that she's running for Congress. I suspect that didn't make everyone happy, but I'm not sure it would rise to the level of murder." He shrugged, "Then again, she's not the only ruthless politician in town."

Coop studied Barry. "Did you notice anyone with her after dessert when she wasn't at her table? Maybe in the hallway near the library or bathroom?"

He shook his head. "Sorry, no. I didn't notice her or anyone else. The only thing I do remember is Joe, her current husband, arrived late. He walked by our table as we were finishing dessert. He nodded at me, and I nodded back, but we didn't speak either."

"Did you and your family play the mystery game?"

"The four guests we had at our table wanted to play, and Bridget did too. I wasn't all that keen on it but encouraged her to go with them. The boys and I stayed behind, although Baron and Adam were getting ready to leave when they asked everyone to stay at their seats so the paramedics could do their work."

Coop shut the cover of his notebook. "Well, I think we'll take you up on seeing if Penelope is home and if Bridget is up to talking with us. With it getting late, we'll try to catch up with Baron and Adam tomorrow."

Barry pulled out his cell phone and after a short conversation, disconnected. "Poppy said to come on by. Bridget's home, and she thinks she's up to a short conversation."

He slipped the phone into his pocket. "Baron works with me at the real estate firm, and he'll be there tomorrow. Adam is tougher to find. He's a doctor at the hospital and works crazy hours, but if you leave him a message, he'll get back to you. If I talk to him, I'll let him know it's urgent." He stood and ushered them to the door.

Coop handed him a business card. "If you remember anything at all about that night at the Sinclairs, give me a call. Sometimes, the small thing unlocks these types of cases."

Barry smiled and took the card. "I'll do that. As much as we struggled in our marriage, I would never wish this on Michelle. I'm also worried about Bridget. Sometimes, it's harder to lose someone you're not close to. Regrets aren't easy companions."

AB and Coop left him with their thanks.

As he walked to the Jeep, Coop raised his brows at AB. "What do you think?"

She shrugged. "He seems sincere. I don't get a vibe that he's lying about anything. Seems to have moved on from their marriage and divorce, but it was clear he wasn't a fan."

"Understandable. I'm not a fan of women who walk out on their kids either." Coop's mind shifted to Marlene. He wondered where his fugitive of a mother was and how long it would be before he heard from her or the jail housing her.

CHAPTER SIX

Coop pushed his mother from his mind and steered the Jeep from Barry's house and back to the main driveway. Less than half a mile away, he caught a glimpse of another stately home and took the turn for Penelope's smaller mansion.

AB parked behind him, and they made their way to the black doors that stood out against the white brick façade. A woman with sandy-blond hair and a warm smile opened the door. She was tall and thin, like her brother, perfectly groomed in a high-end navy suit with a pink blouse. They introduced themselves, and she extended a hand. "I'm Penelope, but everyone calls me Poppy. Please come in."

She led them to a small sitting area just inside the entry nearest the staircase. "Bridget is fetching us some sweet tea. Please have a seat."

Coop and AB sank into one end of the distressed-leather, L-shaped couch, and Poppy sat at the opposite end. "I talked Bridget into going to the gym this morning. Her spirits always seem better after that, but she's struggling to process all of this."

Moments later, a young woman came around the corner, carrying a tray with glasses and a pitcher of tea.

She set the tray on the table, and Poppy poured tea over the ice in the glasses and handed a glass to each of them before taking one for herself. As she managed the tea, Poppy introduced Coop and AB to her niece. Bridget sat next to her aunt, her eyes a match for her dad's. Her long, dark hair were secured in a ponytail. Red blotches under her eyes and around her nose stood out on her pale skin.

Coop took a sip. "Delicious. Thanks so much and thanks for seeing us at this hour. Bridget, we're so very sorry about your mom and just have a few questions for you. We're working for the Sinclairs, the hosts from last night's event."

She nodded, and Poppy reached for her hand.

Coop flicked his gaze to AB, and she set her glass on a coaster. "Your dad tells us you're at Vanderbilt. AB and I both went to college there. What are you studying?"

Bridget's eyes brightened. "Yeah, I like it there. I'm in premed, but I'm not sure I'm going to stay on that track. I'm giving teaching some thought."

Coop nodded. "Bridget, you attended the gala with your dad and his sons last night. Did you have occasion to interact with your mom?"

She shook her head. "No, we were at a different table." She shrugged. "It was really just a chance to dress up, and Dad was excited to go."

AB nodded. "Yes, I had fun dressing up, too. Did you happen to see your mom in the hallway near the library or notice her talking to anyone?"

"I didn't notice anyone but wasn't really paying attention."

Coop reached for his glass. "Where did your clue lead your table to investigate?"

She frowned and tilted her head.

Coop smiled. "You know, the murder mystery game they were hosting with the actors."

"Oh, right. We were supposed to visit the entry hall."

Coop scribbled in his notebook and noticed Bridget picking at the skin around her thumbnails. They were both red and raw.

AB cleared her throat. "Did you happen to use one of the bathrooms in the hallway near the library and music room?"

Bridget's eyes widened. "Oh, yeah, I did. The one in black and white with the checkerboard floor. I spilled a bit of the strawberry sauce on my fingers and needed to wash them and then met up with the others to search the entry."

Coop smiled. "They make the best strawberry shortcake. That was my favorite part of the meal."

Bridget smiled and nodded.

AB continued. "Your dad said you and your mom weren't very close. Had you seen her or talked to her recently?"

Tears filled Bridget's eyes as she shook her head. "No, at Christmas, she talked about us having a girls day at the spa. She and Joe own Zen. I can go whenever I want, but she talked about a whole day of lunch and shopping and different treatments. We just never…" Her voice cracked.

Poppy slipped her arm around her shoulders.

AB softened her voice. "I'm so sorry, Bridget. I know this is difficult. We're just trying to find out what happened. Do you know of anyone who would want to harm your mother or any ongoing problems she was having with anyone?"

She shook her head, her lip quivering. "Not really. She was outspoken, and I've read things in the paper over the years about other politicians having a low opinion of her, but

I don't know of anything recent. Like I said, we didn't talk much. Maxine might know. She's Mom's personal assistant and has been for years."

AB smiled and nodded. "Thanks, Bridget. She's on our list to talk to, so we'll make sure we do." She glanced over at Coop.

He swallowed the last of his tea and set his empty glass on the coaster. "We won't take up any more of your time. Thank you for talking to us."

Penelope patted Bridget's arm. "Why don't you go upstairs? I'll be up to check on you in a few minutes."

Bridget rose and mumbled goodbye before she dashed up the staircase.

Poppy waited a few moments and lowered her voice. "Michelle was a pathetic excuse for a mother. She's the one who had an affair and broke up her marriage to Barry, then she more or less abandoned Bridget. I said good riddance and thought it was a mistake when Barry married her, but at least he got Bridget out of the deal. She's a lovely young woman. A bit self-absorbed but overall, a delight."

With a nod, Coop asked, "Barry said you filled the void when she left and are quite close to Bridget. Did you interact with Michelle much or know anything about her recent activities?"

Her lips formed a thin line. "No, we didn't talk. When she left, I let her know what I thought of her, but since then, I haven't had anything to do with her. Right after the divorce, I was more involved when Bridget was younger, and we tried to encourage Michelle to spend time with her and arrange things, but I haven't talked to her in years. I know nothing about her except what I read in the paper or hear about at the club."

Coop's brows rose. "Any recent rumors at the club?"

Poppy smiled. "Just the general chatter about her making a run for Congress and how she'd fit in better in D.C. with the rest of the swamp creatures. Most everyone would be glad to see her leave Nashville." She sighed. "I try to stay out of it and, for Bridget's sake, don't mention her. She's toyed with Bridget's emotions since the divorce, and I have no respect for her. It's no secret I've never been fond of her, but I wouldn't wish Michelle dead. I worry about Bridget. She's struggling."

"You weren't at the gala last night?" asked Coop.

She shook her head. "No, I went to dinner and a movie with a friend of mine from the tennis club, Roberta Hogan. Barry called me when they learned about Michelle, and I met them at his house and stayed over last night with Bridget. Then, she came over here today."

Coop and AB rose from the couch, and he handed Poppy his business card. "If you think of anything else, or if Bridget remembers anything more about that night at the gala, please get in touch."

She smiled and took the card. "I will, and I'll encourage Bridget to give it more thought and call you if she can remember anything else."

They thanked her and when they were at their vehicles, Coop glanced over at AB. "What's your take on them?"

She shrugged. "Definitely no love lost between Poppy and Michelle, but I can understand it. She had to pick up the slack and help care for Bridget. They're obviously a very close family with them all living here. I feel sorry for the daughter. Like Barry said, she's dealing with regret and guilt, wishing she'd made more of an effort."

After a few moments, Coop nodded. "Yeah, mothers, even the rotten ones, have a hold on their children. I've felt guilty at times for not doing more for my mom and then each time I get involved with her..."

AB shook her head. "You've done more than anybody I know would have for Marlene. I get what you're saying though; we all crave our mother's love, no matter what."

Coop clicked the door open on the Jeep. "Let's call it a night. I'll see you in the morning, and we'll see if we can get in touch with Michelle's coworkers and Barry's two sons. I'm getting a clear picture of her family life, or lack of one, but would like to know more about her work life."

"See you in the morning, Coop." AB raised her hand in a wave and led the way down the road and to the gates of the massive family property.

———

As Coop went through the gates, he slapped the steering wheel. He'd meant to ask Victoria for a tour of the chateau. He wanted a better feel for the rooms and places in the house, especially when asking people their whereabouts during the murder window.

He thought of it when they'd walked through the hallway to the study but had forgotten. He detoured to the Sinclairs, and after pressing the intercom button, he was welcomed once more.

Victoria greeted him at the door and although drained, perked up a bit when he asked her to show him around the house. "I need to get a better idea of the distance between places. We're interviewing guests, and it would be helpful to have a better picture in my mind."

"Of course." She led him through the entry and took a turn that led to a large living area. "We call this the formal living room." She smiled. "We don't use it much." She kept going around a curved hallway and pointed at another room outfitted with couches and chairs and a pool table. "This is the casual space we use most when the kids come to visit. Arthur and I spend most of our time in the small living space you'll see later and of course, the study."

Coop sketched in his notebook as they walked. The hallway continued, and she pointed out a bedroom with a well-appointed bathroom. "This is the only guest room on the main floor."

She led the way across a tiled floor with wooden doors that opened to a portion of the backyard. The space was furnished with two couches and a small table. "This is the sitting room. It has a lovely view of outside. Perfect for reading a book or just gazing."

Past the sitting room was the master suite. It was huge and included a fireplace, along with enough room for the bed, a couch, two chairs, and a wall of bookcases. It also had French doors that led to the patio and pool area. The master bathroom was equally spacious with two walk-in closets that connected the space to the bedroom.

Next came the study, where he and AB had met with the Sinclairs. He pointed at the door on the wall it shared with the master suite. "That connects to your bedroom? Was it locked during the gala?"

Victoria nodded. "Yes, it opens to our master bedroom, which we kept closed during the gala. We did lock that door so guests couldn't access our suite, since the study was a room used for the murder clues."

Coop stepped into the hallway and noted the full bathroom across from the study. It was done in black and white with a checkerboard floor.

Further down was the music room and then the library,

with another full bathroom, this one in soft blues and beiges, at the end of the hallway closest to the library.

The hallway continued where it met up with the Great Hall, and the kitchen was in the area behind the Great Hall, with another living space adjacent to it. Victoria pointed at the couches and the flat-screen TV. "This is where we do most of our living, just the two of us. The other spaces are mostly used when we entertain or have guests. The upper floor was off limits during the gala, and we rarely use it. We do have another master suite upstairs, along with guest bedrooms and another living space."

"You're certain nobody went upstairs?"

She nodded. "We had the elevator locked down, and we had staff stationed at the staircase to deter anyone who might venture past the velvet rope."

"Okay, that helps. Your home is nothing short of spectacular. Thanks for giving me the lay of the land. I'm sorry to bother you so late." Coop walked toward the front entry.

"No need to apologize. I'm impressed you're already working on the case. Camille speaks so highly of you. Now I can see why."

He held up his hand and smiled. "One more quick question. How did you and Arthur feel about Michelle Roberts? Were you supportive of her upcoming campaign for Congress?"

She sighed. "We've always supported the party more than the candidate, especially in the primary. We invited all of them here for the gala to show our support for all of them. We don't decide until closer to the election." She lowered her voice. "Between us, though, she was a little too brash for our taste. Marcus is all talk and very little work. Our support would most likely go to Emily. She's done an excellent job and is more professional. Michelle's nature is more one of recklessness."

"Understood, and it goes nowhere. I was just curious, more than anything."

"Good night, Mr. Harrington."

He descended the steps to his Jeep, lost in thought about how many of the hundreds of people at the gala thought the party was better off without Michelle and who might have taken matters into their own hands to remove her.

CHAPTER SEVEN

C oop was up early on Monday, and he and Gus headed to the office before Camille and Charlie woke. His hope of taking Gus for a walk before work was dashed when he pulled from the garage and rain showered the windshield.

After he parked, they made a quick dash for the door, and Coop used one of the clean towels from the hooks by the back door to dry Gus. He set the coffee to brew, making sure to only portion enough for his large mug before making his way to his office and turning on his computer.

He added the thick file to the conference table and started a few notes on the whiteboard. By the time he was organized, the coffee was ready, and he settled in with his morning infusion of caffeine and studied the guest list, along with his sketch of the chateau from last night and the table layout he got from the caterers on the night of the murder.

From what he knew about succinylcholine, it took effect immediately, so whoever had administered it was someone who wasn't at their table when Michelle was in the library. It also had to be someone she trusted to get close enough to inject her.

That meant family and close colleagues or friends were in the spotlight. He'd also noticed during the event that Michelle was a hugger. She didn't mind if her personal space was invaded and readily invaded that of others she encountered, so he couldn't rule out a mere acquaintance. While Coop was contemplating and still sipping, Gus dashed from his chair and made for the backdoor.

A few minutes later, AB's voice filled the quiet office and when she was done with her morning routine, she came through the door, carrying a cup of tea for herself and a fresh cup of decaf for Coop. She plopped into the chair across from Coop at the conference table.

"Morning," he said, looking up from the guest list.

She took a long swallow from her cup. "I stayed up way too late researching succinylcholine." She confirmed Coop's understanding that it was quick acting and had been used in a few homicides, but wasn't usually detected in the victims due to the fast metabolism of the drug and the fact that most toxicology screenings don't include it, unless there's a reason to suspect it.

AB glanced at her notes. "As far as where to get it, it's used in most medical facilities, primarily as an agent when intubating a patient. Ambulances, paramedics, emergency rooms, care facilities, even veterinarians use it. Like other drugs, it's supposed to be secured and accounted for, but we all know that system isn't foolproof."

Coop's forehead creased. "So, anybody in the medical field would have access, but I don't think we can limit our scope only to those. I can imagine someone might obtain it for another person."

AB nodded. "Yeah, medical related personnel would have

the easiest access, but you're right, it could be procured illegally or stolen or whatever."

Coop pointed at the table layout. "I think our best bet is to try and narrow down the list by figuring out who wasn't at their table when Michelle was in the library." He glanced at his watch. "It's almost eight o'clock. Can you call Michelle's office and get me in to see Maxine, the personal assistant and I'll work on the Marshall brothers and the campaign manager?"

"You got it," said AB, taking her cup and notepad.

Coop had to leave a voicemail for Baron and Adam, but had better luck with the campaign manager, Diane Thornfield, who was willing to see him within an hour. She gave him an address on Church Street.

As Coop was gathering his things, AB came through the door. "Maxine is working out of Michelle's campaign office and she said she'll be there all day. She and Diane were getting it ready to open, but now they're working to shut it down." She handed him a note with the address and Maxine's cell phone number.

He nodded. "Diane is also at that office and can see me at nine-thirty. I'll talk to Maxine while I'm there, too."

"Michelle's state office is in the Cordell Hull Building next to the Capitol. I talked to Candice, who is her administrative assistant. She's a little reluctant, I think, but said she was willing to meet you on her lunch hour. I think she's worried about seeing you at the office." She handed Coop another sticky note with the name of a restaurant he recognized at one of the big hotels on Union Street. "I'll make you a reservation for eleven-thirty."

"Got it, thanks." He stuck the notes inside the cover of his notebook and when he looked up AB was holding his blue sports jacket.

He smiled and slipped it over the button-down shirt he wore. "I thought you'd be proud of me for remembering to wear a real shirt today."

"I am, but you need the jacket. It makes you look more professional."

He slugged down a few more swallows of his coffee, ruffled the top of Gus' head, and said goodbye to him and AB. "I'll call you after lunch and check in. Text me with anything important," he hollered as he rushed out the backdoor.

Downtown was only about ten miles away, but would take at least thirty minutes with traffic and parking would only add to it. By the time he parked and walked to the vintage brick building on Church Street, Coop was ten minutes early.

He took a few minutes to check his messages and email, but found nothing from either Marshall brother. He took the stairs to the second-floor suite and opened the unmarked wooden door with only the suite number noted above it.

Tables and desks were scattered in the open space, with boxes stacked upon them. Signs in red, white, and blue urging voters to cast their vote for Roberts for Congress were scattered about and leaning against the walls. Michelle's motto was restoring accountability and integrity and was emblazoned on her campaign materials.

As Coop was surveying the space, a woman with short dark hair streaked with gray came from the back of the office. She was on her phone and jumped when she noticed him. She smiled and held up her finger.

After wrapping up her call, the petite woman hurried toward Coop, her hand extended. "So sorry, Mr. Harrington. I'm Diane Thornfield. Sorry to keep you waiting."

He shook her hand. "No problem. I'm a few minutes early."

She waved her hand over the space. "Please excuse this mess. We were in the midst of getting things organized for Michelle with her announcement to run for Congress last week." She shook her head. "Now, we have to dismantle everything and shut it down."

After a few moments of her staring at the table covered in boxes, she gestured for Coop to follow her. "Come on back. Would you like coffee or water?"

He held up his hand. "No, thanks, I'm good."

She slipped behind her desk and he took the chair in front of it. "First, I'm sorry for your loss. I think you've been with Michelle since her first foray into the political arena."

She nodded. "Yes, we've worked together for years, so it's been difficult and shocking."

He took his notebook from his pocket. "As I explained, I'm working for the Sinclairs, who are understandably worried and upset about the crime taking place at their home. They're hoping I can assist in apprehending the suspect quickly and rest assured I work closely with the police."

She winked at him. "I did a little research on you this morning and am comfortable speaking with you and helping in any way I can. You have a stellar reputation."

Coop grinned and poised his pen on his pad. "Good to know. I'm interested in when Michelle left your table at the gala and where she was going."

Diane nodded. "Right. As I remember, it was during the production with the actors and the murder mystery, right before it ended. I assumed she was going to the restroom. She didn't have a big interest in playing the game with the mystery. We were there for the campaign and to work the room, as they say, for donors."

"Had she had any recent threats or problems with anyone at the gala? Does anyone come to mind that would want to harm her?"

Her jaw tightened. "Michelle was not the easiest person. She'd made some enemies throughout her career and her whole campaign for Congress was focused on revealing corruption and waste. She's ruffled feathers here with the things she's uncovered in Tennessee and vowed to do the same at the national level."

Coop nodded. "Obviously, she's a threat to sitting Congressman Marcus Ryle and she and Emily Harper are rivals. I've heard she had plans to expose someone in the party. Her party."

She bobbed her head and positioned her tablet in front of Coop. "In fact, she just sent this out late Friday night to several journalists and podcasters. It's an audio recording of Randy Boone, the state party chair, visiting her several weeks ago and begging her not to run for Congress. Going so far as asking what her price would be to step away and take a job on a board of a company. She could name what she wanted. He was delivering a message from DC. The mainstream media aren't touching it yet, but they will soon."

She hit the button and Coop listened to the exchange. His brows rose as Michelle told Randy she couldn't be bought and wanted to know who specifically sent him. He wouldn't answer and intimated he was at risk if she even mentioned their conversation.

The hint of a smile on Diane's face faded and she lowered her voice. "Marcus is livid. Emily is popular and was considered a threat to him, but Michelle could be a bigger one, to both of them. Randy Boone, though, he's beside himself. He's the head of the party here in Tennessee and has been working to undermine Michelle's ambitions. Along with releasing this audio, her plans included publicizing the money he's wasted on what most would say are personal luxuries and expenses, while denying Michelle support for her bid for Congress. It was getting nasty."

Coop wrote down his name. "He was at the gala that night. I remember seeing his name."

Diane nodded. "Yes, he was sitting with Marcus. He's made it clear the party plans to protect his seat."

"What about Michelle's husband, Joe?"

She shrugged. "I don't think they're a great match for each other. When they met he had a gym and she's transformed that business and bankrolled it into Zen, which is profitable and popular. She doesn't tell me much about her personal life, but I get the feeling he wasn't happy with her quest for Congress. He's not around much, usually spends his time at Zen. She was frustrated with him and his lack of experience or seriousness, whatever you want to call it, when it came to the business. He's sort of a blow-hard. Likes to talk more than work."

"I know he arrived late to the gala. Was he at the table the entire time, after he arrived?"

Her forehead creased. "Yes, I think so. He came in when they were serving dessert and when she left, he was still there. I wasn't playing the game either. Maxine, Michelle, and I were planning to huddle with Mr. Winters, her biggest donor. The only people playing from our table were Doris, she's Anthony Carlisle's wife, and my husband, Mike. They had no interest in spending time listening to political strategy." She laughed and reached for her cup of coffee.

"Eliza was Michelle's attorney and Anthony Carlisle was Michelle's business partner?"

She nodded. "That's right. Eliza was her long-time attorney. Anthony was the main investor in Zen and helped Michelle get on her feet after her divorce from Barry Marshall."

Coop added more notes in his notebook. "So, Michelle left the table first, then Doris and Mike left after the staged murder and everyone else stayed at the table and never left?"

Diane moved her reading glasses atop her head. "That's right. I remember waiting for Michelle to get back. Our web designer had just sent through the draft site so we could approve it and I had texted her after she left. It looked great and I knew she'd be excited to see it. I was scrolling through it at the table when Victoria announced the paramedics were on site and asked everyone to go back to their tables."

Coop asked her to check the time she texted Michelle and he added 8:12 to his notebook. He then asked her for the contact information for the others at the table.

She scrolled through her phone and wrote down the information he needed for the spouses of those in attendance. "I know you have to check them out, but I can say without a reservation, none of them would be involved with killing Michelle."

Coop put the paper she gave him in his notebook and rose. "I understand. I'm just checking everything and more than anything looking for perspectives. Different people notice different things and sometimes that leads to a breakthrough." He reached for the door. "Thank you for your time. I'm supposed to meet Maxine here, too."

Diane rose and followed him out the door. "She should be here by now. Her office is just down the hall."

They took several steps and followed the curve of the hallway where Diane rapped her knuckles on a closed wooden door before cracking it open.

A woman with short red hair sat at desk, focused on the screen of her computer. "Maxine, Mr. Harrington is here."

The woman with black and white polka dot cat-eye glasses turned to face them. She rose from her chair and offered Coop a seat. Her face was quite pale underneath the cap of deep red hair. "Thanks, Diane," said Maxine, with a slight dismissive tone.

Coop thanked her for seeing him and settled into the cushioned chair. "I'm just gathering a bit of background information and I'm most interested in your thoughts of who might have wanted to harm Michelle?"

She shook her head. "She had more than a few political enemies, but it's hard to imagine they would kill her, although releasing that audio was risky. Michelle was fearless when it came to those things. Sunlight was the best thing for corruption, she always said."

"Of those at the gala, does anyone come to mind? Did you notice anyone following her when she left your table?"

"I didn't notice anyone, but I wasn't paying attention. I'm sure Diane's told you about Marcus Ryle and Randy Boone being upset with Michelle and her bid for Congress. I'm sure Emily wasn't happy either, but she wasn't one to make a public fuss. Again, I can't say they would be capable of murder, but they had the most to lose and the audio was damning. Now, with her death, it will be even more salacious."

"What about her personal life?"

Maxine sighed. "Michelle was very focused on her career, so oftentimes her personal and familial relationships suffered. There was tension between her and Joe, but again, I can't see him killing her."

"Was there infidelity involved?"

Her cheeks reddened. "All this digging around, you're

bound to turn it up. She was certain Joe was stepping out on her with Paula Kinkade. She's the manager of Zen in Green Hills. Joe's supposed to manage the Franklin site, where he and Michelle live, but she became suspicious when he was spending more and more time in Green Hills. He denied it, but she was certain."

As he was writing, Maxine continued. "She also had a number of private meetings with Daniel Prescott."

Coop's brow furrowed. "As in Governor Brown's Chief of Staff?"

"Correct. I can't say with certainty and did my best to stay out of Michelle's personal life, but I know the difference between a professional or business relationship and one that crosses the line. I tried to suggest she limit her interactions so as not to give her opponents any ammunition against her, but she bit my head off and denied any wrongdoing." She shrugged. "I could be wrong, but I'm pretty certain there was more to their relationship."

Coop finished his notes and met Maxine's eyes. "I gather Michelle and her daughter weren't close."

Maxine frowned and bit her lip. "It was sad. Bridget was devastated when her parents divorced. She blamed Michelle and honestly, it was her fault. She was having an affair. Bridget wanted to stay with Barry and that seemed to work for Michelle. She was my friend, but she had her shortcomings. Her maternal instincts were non-existent. I tried to encourage her to do more with Bridget and schedule lunches and fun days with her, but Michelle always found an excuse to work instead. Poppy, her aunt, has been more like a mom to her than Michelle was."

Tears filled her eyes and she reached for a tissue. "Michelle had her faults, but she was excellent at her job and was brave when it came to rooting out corruption and waste and confronting lots of the good old boys in government. I don't want to paint her in a bad light, but I know you need the truth if you're going to find her killer."

"I appreciate that and I'm not here to judge. It all helps me get a picture of her and consider possible motives. I can tell it's not easy for you and I admire your candor."

After thanking her, he left her with his card and asked her to pass one to Diane in case either of them thought of anything else that might help.

He left their office and walked to the restaurant, his mind reeling with the revelations about Michelle's personal life. He and AB would need to brainstorm the best approach when it came to approaching the husband, not to mention the man who had the ear of the governor.

Coop hoped Candice didn't have anything else to add to the political bonfire Michelle had started. He already had plenty of gas to throw on it.

CHAPTER EIGHT

L ess than an hour later, under a gloomy and overcast
sky, Coop left Candice at the corner and as he walked
to the parking garage, pulled out his cell phone. "Hey, AB,
just finished up lunch. Have you heard from anyone else?"

"Baron called and said he's available at four o'clock today.
No word from Adam yet."

"Okay, I'll be back to the office in thirty minutes. I
learned quite a bit from Diane and Maxine and need to
brainstorm with you."

He slipped the phone back in his pocket, retrieved the
Jeep, and headed back to his office. As he was driving, his cell
rang. He hit the button to connect via Bluetooth.

"Mr. Harrington, this is Darcy Flint. I'm calling about
your mother."

Coop's shoulders tensed as he listened to her explain
Marlene had been arrested in another town in Vermont and
as her lawyer, she was contacted when the system flagged an
outstanding warrant. "Our police here will be extraditing her
back to serve her sentence. I just wanted you to know."

Coop sighed, certain his mother was on earth only to test his patience. His was running low when it came to Marlene and her antics. "Thanks, Ms. Flint. I appreciate the call. I think we'll just let the system take its course with her. At this point, there's no point in defending her. She can use a public defender. The result will be the same in that she'll be incarcerated for violating her release conditions. Sadly, jail is where she belongs."

"I understand and agree. I just wanted you to know, at this point, she'll have to face the full sentence. The judge isn't likely to offer any leniency after her disappearing act. If I learn anything new, I'll let you know."

He thanked her again and disconnected.

His head pounded, and he was sure his blood pressure was off the charts. He cracked the window and let the cool air wash over him. As he took the turn for his office, he wondered how long it would be before he'd get a collect call from a jail in Vermont.

Gus met him at the back door, his tail wagging and his eyes full of concern. His loyal dog never failed to amaze him with his keen ability to know when Coop needed him most. He bent down, gave his furry friend some scratches behind his ears, and ran his hand down Gus' silky back. "You're a good boy."

Coop made his way to AB's desk with Gus at his side. She turned from her computer screen and frowned. "What's wrong?"

He slumped into the chair nearest her desk. "Got a call from Darcy Flint. Seems like Marlene found herself in more trouble. She was arrested in another town, and the outstanding warrant came up. She'll be extradited back to the jurisdiction she fled. What a mess."

AB's jaw tightened. "Well, I can't say I'm surprised. You said it was only a matter of time."

He nodded as he petted Gus' head. "Yep, I know. She's such a disappointment and while jail is where she belongs, I can't help but feel guilty for being glad my mom is locked in a cell in Vermont."

"Coop, you've got no reason to feel guilty. You've done everything you can for her. She's her own worst enemy and is the cause of all her problems and drama."

He blew out a breath. "Yeah, I know all that. It's like what we were talking about with Michelle and Bridget. No matter how bad your parents are, there's something embedded deep inside that makes a kid long for their approval and their love. I know it doesn't make sense. I just wish Marlene would get her act together and not drag me into her mess."

"You mentioned drama. We both know she thrives on it and craves the attention it brings. On the bright side, she'll be occupied for the next month or two, right? I'm going to choose to look at the positive, and that's a definite plus."

Coop chuckled. "You're right, AB. As usual. It just caught me off guard. I'll shake off the funk, I promise."

She patted her hands on her thighs. "That's more like it. Now, what did you learn?"

He rose from the chair, and she followed him into his office, where he sat at the conference table. "I'll start with the boring bits first. In talking with Candice, it was apparent Michelle wasn't well-liked at the office. She left me with the impression most of the staff feared her. She did say that Michelle was strict about keeping her campaign tasks separate from her state position she's serving in now. Candice said she was very demanding of staff and pushed them hard. Wasn't winning many friends there, but also didn't socialize with them. They all felt it was just a stepping stone for her political career, and she was most interested in finding problems and magnifying them for her political use." AB took a sip from her cup. "Sounds like there won't be too many people mourning her passing at the office."

"Exactly. None of them attended the gala. From what Candice says, none of them were close to her. She ran a tight ship, was a perfectionist, and expected the same from everyone who worked with her. Candice did point out that she was generous when it came to treating them to takeout and expensive holiday gifts, but Michelle was an equal opportunity antagonist when it came to scrutinizing state and local governments. Candice couldn't think of anyone work related who would target Michelle. She was known to go after all the departments with equal gusto, so she wasn't winning friends in that area either."

He went to the whiteboard. "Sounds like the people who had the most to lose from Michelle's run and forthcoming disclosure of shenanigans in the party are Marcus Ryle and Randy Boone, along with Emily Harper. We already had them on our radar, but I learned Michelle sent an audio to a few alternative news outlets. It was a recording of Randy offering her a bribe to step away from her race for Congress."

AB's eyes widened. "Wowza. I would imagine when the news gets out she was murdered, that's going to get dicey."

Coop nodded. "I want to let Ben know about it in case it's news to him."

He paused and picked up a marker. "Along with that firestorm, we have a new name to add to our list of persons of interest." He added Daniel Prescott's name to the board and watched AB's eyebrows arch.

"As in Governor Brown's?"

Coop nodded. "Yes, that one." He paused and added,

"Maxine suspects he and Michelle were involved romantically."

"Whoa," said AB. "One of Nashville's most eligible bachelors. He was at the gala with others from Governor Brown's inner circle."

Coop nodded. "I know. The problem is how to question him without creating a hullaballoo." He wrote one more name on the list. "I also learned that Michelle was convinced Paula Kinkade, who manages the Green Hills location of Zen, and her husband were having an affair."

AB's brows rose even higher. "Holy cow." She quickly scanned the guest list and shook her head. "She's not on the list."

"I don't think she's in the same social circles as those we met at the gala. Remember, Joe was very late getting there. Makes me wonder where he was, but both Diane and Maxine are sure he didn't leave the table when Michelle was gone. They assumed she was visiting the ladies room, as none of them were participating in trying to solve the murder mystery game. They were talking strategy."

"Hmm," AB muttered as she studied the board. "I'll dig into her and see what I can find out. I did contact Poppy's tennis friend, and she confirmed they were together at dinner and the theater during the timeframe of the murder."

"Also, we need to talk to Anthony Carlisle, his wife, Eliza Dugan, and Diane's husband, Mike. They were all at Michelle's table, and the spouses were playing the game, so they took their envelope and went in search of clues. It's a long shot that they were involved, but we need to clear them from the list. Jonathan Winters is another name they dropped. He's a big donor."

AB nodded and penned a note on her pad. "I'll do some research on him and see what I can set up with the others."

She glanced up at Coop. "Oh, Camille called and invited me to join you guys for Sunday supper on Monday."

He chuckled. "Sounds good to me. After my day, I could use some of her comfort food. I'll swing by Baron's office and call it a day. Do you mind giving Gus a ride home when you leave?"

The dog raised his head from the leather chair where he was snoozing. She smiled at him and said, "Sure thing. We'll meet you at the house."

———

Coop had to leave a voicemail for Ben to let him know about Michelle's audio release before he turned his attention to the background reports AB had prepared for both Marshall brothers. Satisfied there wasn't anything in either that raised a red flag, outside of Adam's work in the medical field, he set out for Baron's office in Green Hills. Coop pulled to the curb in front of a historic stone cottage that served as the offices of the Marshall Group.

The yard and exterior were immaculate and inviting. A friendly woman at a reception desk greeted him and led him to Baron's corner office, situated with a view of the backyard.

Baron came from behind the desk and welcomed Coop with a firm handshake and a smile. "Mr. Harrington, please have a seat."

The receptionist appeared with a tray of coffee and tea and without AB there to supervise, Coop happily accepted the cup of steaming dark brew. "Thanks for making the time for me today. I'm interested in anything you noticed the night of the gala. For instance, did anyone leave your table after dessert? Who from your group was participating in the murder mystery game?"

His forehead creased, and he paused for a few moments. "The only one I remember leaving from our table was Bridget. She needed to visit the restroom after dessert. Our table was the four of us and then two of our agents, Aly and Matt, and their spouses."

Baron flipped the pen he held between his fingers. "Adam and I weren't interested in the game. I don't think Dad was either, but Bridget acted like she wanted to play. He encouraged her to go with the other four who were all over the idea of finding clues."

"Do you remember where the envelope directed them?" asked Coop, as he added notes to his notepad.

With a shake of his head, Baron said, "No, sorry. I didn't pay attention. I had a call from my girlfriend and stepped away to the patio to talk when that all started, so I wasn't involved. Adam and I were both ready to leave and were discussing it, until Victoria announced the emergency and asked everyone to take their seats."

Coop took a swallow of coffee. "Your dad told us the divorce wasn't exactly amicable, but he and Michelle had come to terms with it over the years. Did you have any contact with Michelle?"

He shook his head and laughed. "Not if I could help it. She was horrible to Dad and never nice to me or Adam. She was a gold digger. Dad was vulnerable after losing Mom, and she took advantage of him, in my opinion. Then he had to pay a fortune to get rid of her in the divorce. I couldn't stand her and her phony schtick about exposing corruption and waste. I'm not overly involved in politics, but she doesn't strike me as the best spokesmodel for that. Not from what I've seen of her personally."

He paused and took a deep breath. "Sorry, all that to say, I think there's a long list of people she's stepped on over the years or screwed over. I didn't like her at all but wouldn't kill her. I imagine it must be someone with stronger feelings than me or someone threatened by her."

Coop nodded. "I agree. Right now, we're at the stage of trying to paint a picture of who in her life would take that step, and our list of suspects includes the two hundred people on the guest list at the gala. I'm just asking questions of those who knew her, like you and your brother."

"As much as I hated her, I would never ruin my life or my family's for someone like her. She's not worth the effort. She's done enough to our family already." He glanced at his cell phone vibrating atop his desk. "Adam is coming by here, along with my girlfriend. She's a songwriter, and Adam met her as a patient and then introduced us. Turns out her sister works at Vanderbilt too. We're going to dinner. If you have the time, I'm sure Adam can spare a few minutes to talk to you while you're here."

"Oh, that would be great. It won't take long."

Baron rose and stepped toward the door. "I'll send him in as soon as he gets here. His text said he was just down the street." He left the room and left the door open.

Coop circled the note he added to his list about Adam working at the hospital and Baron's girlfriend's sister. They'd both have access to the drug that killed Michelle and know how to administer it.

As he took another sip from his cup, Baron walked back into the office with another man, who he introduced to Coop as Adam. "I'll leave you to it," he said and clicked the door closed behind him.

Adam shook Coop's hand and slid into the chair next to him. "Sorry, I haven't had a chance to get back to you. My work schedule is pretty nuts. Baron said you're looking into Michelle's murder."

Coop nodded. "That's right. Hoping to collect any observations or knowledge you might have about the incident that night."

Adam's eyes widened. "I didn't talk to her and haven't talked to her for a very long time. None of us have a close, or what you would call warm, relationship with her. We do our best not to disparage her in front of Bridget, but she's not part of our lives. Hasn't been for a very long time."

"We're just trying to get a picture of where everyone was after dessert. Did you or anyone else leave the table at any time?"

Adam frowned and paused in thought. "I remember Bridget had some strawberry sauce on her hands so she went to wash up right after the murder scene. I wasn't interested in playing the game and dashed to the bar to grab another drink for me and one for Dad. When I got back to the table, Baron was coming in from outside, and Dad was there alone. The other four were playing the game, and they'd already left to find their clue."

"You're a doctor at Vanderbilt?"

He nodded. "Yeah, ER resident at the moment. I'm considering moving over to the surgical center though. Better schedule there."

"Oh, I've had a couple of trips to the ER. Kidney stone was the most memorable."

"Ooh, yeah. Those are rough. I like the fast pace that comes from the ER and helping people, but it's really tough lately. We're understaffed and overrun."

"Baron said you introduced him to his girlfriend and work with her sister at the hospital."

Adam smiled. "Yes, I introduced him to Carina. She's

great. Her sister Deb is a colleague. She's an anesthesiologist and is encouraging me to give the surgical center or a specialty route consideration."

"Do you have any thoughts on anyone you saw at the gala that night that could have killed Michelle?"

Adam shook his head. "I don't socialize much, so I couldn't tell you who most of the people in the room were. I recognized a few politicians from the newspaper and news, but I don't know enough about any of them to comment on their feelings toward Michelle."

"If I told you she was killed with succinylcholine, would that prompt a different answer?"

His blue eyes widened. "Wow, that's surprising." He paused and added, "I can see why you're interested in those of us in the medical field. It's a specialized drug and mainly used for intubation or surgical procedures."

Coop's forehead wrinkled. "Would you have to have much medical training to administer it?"

"Not necessarily. I mean, yes for surgical procedures, but if you're just stabbing someone with it, not really. It's usually given in an IV but can be given intramuscularly. Usually in the hip or upper arm or even the buttocks. If you're not worried about the patient or outcome, it would just be a thrust of a needle. It takes very little time to act."

"If given a fatal dose, how long would it take for the person to die?"

Adam sighed. "Minutes. It's very quick acting, which is why it's used for intubation. It's a paralytic that takes only seconds to work when given intravenously, and it clears the body very quickly. It would be a matter of minutes if you were given an overdose." He shook his head. "She would have been awake but unable to move. I guess it would be a blessing that it only takes minutes, but it would feel longer, I'm sure."

Coop made another note. "From what I know, it's used in lots of medical settings. Would it be hard to come by for an average person not part of the medical community?"

"Gosh, I would hope so. It's a staple in most emergency rooms, ambulances, long-term-care institutions, veterinary clinics, surgical suites, of course. It's not as secure as I like to think, considering when you need it, you need it quickly. But drugs are monitored closely in all those places I mentioned."

Coop closed his notebook. "Obviously, this was a well-thought-out plan. Premeditated, as we lawyers like to say. Someone had access to the drug and plotted Michelle's murder. We just need to find out who."

CHAPTER NINE

After meeting Carina and thanking the brothers, Coop left them to their dinner plans and drove home. As he pulled into the driveway, he noticed AB's Beetle was there. As he made his way to the house, the exhaustion of the day slowed his pace. The anticipation of the inevitable call he'd get from his mother weighed on him.

As soon as he opened the door, Gus was there to greet him, tail wagging. He always lifted Coop's spirits. His furry sidekick followed him into the kitchen, where Camille was busy prepping. and AB and Charlie were seated at the island counter.

Camille looked up from the salad she was making. "You look tired, Coop. Are you feeling okay?"

"It's been a long day." He slid into the chair between his dad and AB. Camille poured him some iced tea and added a splash of lemonade. "There you go. Drink that up and relax."

He took a long swallow and savored the refreshing taste.

"How did your interview go?" asked AB.

"Good. Adam also showed up, so I talked to him, too.

Baron, the oldest, shares Poppy's feelings about Michelle. He had no use for her. Adam echoed some of the same opinions, but he's not as bitter. Baron's girlfriend is a songwriter, and her sister works at the hospital with Adam as an anesthesiologist."

AB's eyebrows arched. "Both interesting and inconvenient considering the weapon." She hurried from her chair to help Camille with the scalloped potato dish and the rolls just coming out of the oven.

Coop shrugged. "Interesting, but it also reminded me of how many people are connected to the hospital and medical field around here. Vanderbilt is such a huge employer. I bet half the people on the guest list have some sort of tangential relationship to someone in medicine that could have access to the drug."

Everyone pitched in and helped carry items to the table, and then they all sat for a meal resembling Aunt Camille's Easter dinner. As they passed platters, Coop glanced over at his dad. "I got a call about Mom today. She's been arrested again."

Camille gasped. "What in tarnation has she done now?"

Charlie shook his head. "I'm sorry, son. I wish you didn't have to deal with her."

"Her lawyer called me, but I expect a call from Marlene soon. I don't think it will take long to get her extradited back to the little town she was in before."

AB cleared her throat. "Actually, she called while you were out this afternoon. Collect, of course. I went ahead and took the call. She, as we predicted, wanted you and said this was her only call, and you needed to fix the situation for her. She didn't belong in jail... blah, blah, blah."

Camille rolled her eyes. "That woman. She's infuriatin' and awful."

AB met Coop's eyes. "I probably shouldn't have said anything more, but I let her know you wouldn't be paying for an attorney since she had violated the terms of her release and that she could request a public defender, but she should prepare herself for the full force of the law and the sentence that would be imposed." She sighed. "Sorry if I overstepped. I figured they wouldn't let her call again and thought it would save time to just tell her like it is and be done with her."

Coop grinned, surprised at the relief he felt. "Aww, you did fine, AB. Saved me a struggle session with her. I don't envy the jailer who has to deal with her for the next month or however long she gets. If she acts like she did before, I suspect the judge will slap on more time."

Charlie put down his fork. "On the bright side, at least she'll be out of your hair and you'll know where she is. We don't have to worry about her if she's in jail."

As Coop dug into the creamy potatoes, he caught his dad's eye. "That part is good. I do worry about her and the way she lives. Like I was telling AB, she makes me so mad, I can't see straight. But at the same time, I feel guilty or sad or whatever."

Charlie shook his head. "You've got to remember, Coop, she's a master manipulator. She does a great job of twisting people up and dragging them into whatever mess she's made. I tried, to no avail, to fix things and fix her for years. She's got to want to fix herself, and you just need to let her be. I bet you only hear from her when she needs something, right?"

With a heavy heart, Coop nodded. "Yeah, that's been the routine for years now."

Charlie shoulders sagged. "She never calls your brother. Any guesses why?"

With a tsk, Camille put down her glass. "Because Jack doesn't have the means to pay for lawyers, hotels, tickets, or fines. He's not a lawyer who can help her navigate the legal system. Bottom line, Coop, Marlene is a self-absorbed narcissist, and all she does is use anyone she can for her benefit. She loves nobody but herself."

By the time she finished her tirade, Coop noticed his aunt's hands shaking. He reached over and put his hand on her arm. "You're right, Aunt Camille. I think sometimes, I just keep hoping she'll change and dealing with her brings up lots of old emotions."

Camille's eyes filled with tears, and she patted Coop's hand. "I'm sorry, Coop. She brings out the worst in me. People like her don't deserve two lovely sons like you and Jack. After all these years, I hate that she has the power to bring chaos to your life."

Charlie dabbed a napkin at his mouth. "I think it's best we relegate Marlene to the back of our minds. She's sucked enough of our energy and time over the last several months."

Coop raised his glass of tea. "Here, here. I promise I'm done dredging up bad memories. Let's focus on the murder instead."

Camille and Charlie chuckled as they both raised their glasses with AB and toasted to changing the subject to something happier, like Coop's current murder case.

"We're dealing with a very small murder window. We found Michelle at 8:27 that night. When I talked with her campaign manager, she'd texted Michelle, who had left the table a few minutes before, at 8:12. So, we're talking a matter of fifteen or twenty minutes from the time she left her table until we found her in the library."

AB gazed across the table, lost in thought. "When we talked to the actors and others that night, we were confident they had finished their scene at eight fifteen. They had it planned and hit their mark."

As Coop explained more about the drug used to murder Michelle, Camille gasped. "How horrific."

"Right? It shuts down all your muscle activity, so no more breathing, but your eyes stay open. It would be brutal for the minutes it would take to die. You'd be powerless to get help."

When they finished eating, AB volunteered to clear the dishes. While she stacked them, she said, "So the theory is somebody took a syringe full of this stuff to the gala with the intent of killing Michelle. When she was alone in the library, they took their opportunity, injected her, and escaped back to the party. On the surface, that doesn't seem like an amateur. I'd be a wreck if I had a syringe of that stuff in my pocket."

Coop frowned. "Yeah, I would think the murderer would be on edge with something like that on them. Then, they'd also have to get it out of the house. Of course, nobody suspected that initially since it looked more like a heart attack or possible poisoning from the champagne glass."

Camille shook her head. "I guess the police should have searched everyone before releasing us."

As Coop handed AB his plate, he grimaced. "That would be hard to do, especially in a room full of high-powered politicians with lawyers on speed dial or sitting right next to them."

Camille nodded. "I did hear they're having a celebration of life gathering for Michelle at Zen in Green Hills next week."

Coop's brows rose. "I was pondering the idea of having AB go to Zen and do a little sleuthing, posing as a prospective client or member." He caught AB's eye from across the table. "Are you up for that? Maybe later this week?

I'm hoping you can get a feel for the rumor about Paula and Joe being an item."

"Sure, I can handle that."

Camille glanced over at Coop. "I've got peach cobbler for dessert."

"Oh, count me in for that," said Charlie, before Coop could answer.

He grinned at his aunt and pointed at his dad. "What he said and with ice cream."

———

Tuesday morning, after reading the sensationalized headlines about Michelle's murder and the details of the audio recording she released, which was now in all the mainstream news, Coop put a call into Lois Evans, and she agreed to stop by his office to talk later in the day. With that item off his list, he checked his notes from last night's conversation with Ben.

His old friend called while they were eating dessert to let Coop know he got his message about Michelle's release of the bribery audio. He knew about it but thanked Coop. Ben also confirmed that they did sweep the chateau for the murder weapon, even going so far as to collect and examine the trash the caterers transported from the event. There was no sign of a syringe or vial.

Coop shared what he'd learned about Joe having an affair with the manager of Zen in Green Hills and the rumor about Michelle and Daniel Prescott. Ben couldn't talk long but promised to see him Friday morning at Peg's.

As he pondered the white board, AB came into his office. He pointed at the names on the board. "There are so many suspects, this is driving me mad. So far, I've got Adam,

Baron, and Bridget on the list of those who were missing from their table at the time of the murder. Of course, the two real estate agents and their spouses, who were playing the murder game, were also gone."

He pointed at another column. "I left the spouses at Michelle's table who were playing the game on the suspect list, but I have my doubts that any of them would have a motive. We'll need to eliminate them and account for their whereabouts. I also need you to check the footage to see if Baron was indeed on the patio on his phone. Adam says he was at the bar and then back at their table. Bridget was washing her hands and then went with the others to play the game."

AB nodded. "We'll need to figure out where those in your other column were during the time window. We know it only took minutes, so the window is small and will be hard to pinpoint. Daniel Prescott, the governor's main guy and possible secret lover of the victim. Marcus Ryle, a powerful politician whose seat Michelle was threatening. Randy Boone, the leader of the party and the man who was trying to bribe Michelle to stop her campaign for Congress. Those are three we need to figure out soon."

Coop circled their names in red. "Not to mention, Emily Harper, who is Michelle's current rival in her party, both vying for Marcus' seat in Congress."

AB slid a folder over to him. "Here are the interview questions I worked on for the guests at Michelle's table. Hopefully, the spouses who were playing the game can help corroborate the whereabouts of the others and if they were always together, we should be able to eliminate them quickly. Same with the real estate group."

Coop glanced at his watch. "Soon, we'll see what Mr. Carlisle has to add. From what we've learned, he's known

Michelle a long time. Hopefully, he'll be able to shed some light on all of this."

After Coop reviewed the interview questions AB prepared for the guests at Michelle's table, he tidied his desk in preparation for Anthony Carlisle's arrival, Michelle's longtime business partner. He came through the door right on time, and Coop welcomed him to a chair, while AB delivered his requested glass of sweet tea.

Gus greeted him with a wagging tail, and Anthony scratched him behind the ears before Coop pointed to the dog's chair, and Gus hopped up onto it. Gus was an excellent judge of character and the fact that he took a liking to Anthony made Coop think he was most likely a good guy.

Coop chatted with him for a few minutes, basking in his slow Southern drawl, and learned Carlisle was an investor in many local businesses. Done with the small talk, Coop launched into his questions related to Michelle's death. Anthony never left the table after dessert and was talking with Diane, Maxine, Joe, and Eliza while they waited for Michelle to return. He confirmed the others were playing the game and went in search of clues.

"Do you have any theories about who killed Michelle?"

Anthony's jaw clenched. "I'm sure by now you've heard that Michelle could be difficult. She was tough and very focused. She always said if she were a man, she would have been praised, but being a woman, she was judged sometimes quite harshly. She was no shrinking violet when it came to her pursuit of those in the political arena involved in corruption or unethical activities."

"So, you're thinking someone in her political life?"

He shrugged. "That would be my guess. She told me she was releasing a damning audio clip of Randy." Anthony shook his head. "I told her it was risky. Randy is a powerful player with lots of connections beyond Tennessee."

He took a sip of his tea and chuckled. "Michelle was fearless. She kicked lots of hornets' nests in her time and in a way, she relished it. This, though, was a whopper of a nest."

"How about her husband Joe? Did they have a good marriage?"

Anthony rolled his eyes. "I think they had what I would call a fiery relationship. When they were happy, they were both on cloud nine, but lately, there'd been more bad patches than happy ones. When Michelle decided to run for Congress, she signed over her controlling interest in Zen to me. She wanted to divest herself of any direct business holdings, so she'd be above scrutiny. If, and when, she got out of politics, I'd sign her share back to her. She didn't trust Joe with it, and I really didn't trust him when it came to business decisions. She knew I'd keep the business in the black."

Coop jotted a note. "So, he's not the best businessman?"

Anthony laughed. "Not at all. The gym he had was floundering. He treated it like a hobby. He likes to work out, bought the gym, which wasn't much, from the guy who had it. He was making payments to him and renting the location in a strip mall. Anyway, when he and Michelle got together, I think she wanted something for him to do that he enjoyed and came up with the idea of Zen, incorporating the gym part but expanding it to wellness and spa treatments, where there was way more money to be made. Also, she targeted the upscale clientele and designed Zen to cater to them. She is—I mean—*was* brilliant in both politics and business. She had the gift of being able to see ahead."

Coop noticed Anthony's voice cracked when he spoke about Michelle in the past tense. "Do you think their bad patches in their marriage could escalate to Joe killing her?"

With wide eyes, Anthony shook his head. "I can't see it. This will sound bad, but he's not industrious enough to undertake something like that. He's got it made. He doesn't work too hard, makes a good living, and enjoys a nice life with Michelle. No real responsibilities. Life will be harder for him without her." He shrugged. "But I don't know him as well as I knew Michelle."

"If you were to guess, it sounds like you think Randy is the most likely suspect?"

He held up his hands. "Now, I'm not saying he did it. I just think it makes the most sense. His life is easier *without* Michelle. She was a disrupter to the old guard. She was shaking things up in the party and making the status quo uncomfortable. He and others didn't like that."

"One more question, Anthony. I've uncovered a rumor that Joe was stepping out on Michelle with a woman named Paula Kinkade. She's the manager of the Green Hills Zen location."

Anthony's eyebrows arched. "Hmm, well, I'm not involved in the day-to-day operations of the locations. I've met Paula a time or two but don't know anything about an affair. Michelle never mentioned it, and she was pretty forthcoming with me."

"How about on Michelle's part? Was she faithful to Joe?"

Anthony shrugged. "There were always rumors about Michelle. She cheated on Barry, and while I loved Michelle and considered her a close friend, I wasn't blind to her faults. I don't know of any current affairs, but it's not to say she wasn't involved with someone else. She didn't always see her own flaws in that area."

Coop thanked him for his time and when he handed Anthony his card, he let him know he'd be reaching out to his wife for a quick interview to get her observations about the evening of the murder.

They shook hands, and Coop led him to the door and then sank into the couch in the reception area next to AB's desk.

AB glanced over at him. "Lois is due here in a few minutes, and Camille dropped off some of her chocolate chunk cookies with pecans."

He leapt from the couch and bolted for the kitchen in search of an afternoon pick-me-up in the form of a delicious and fresh cookie. He smiled as he took one from the glass platter he recognized. It was still warm. His aunt knew exactly how to help heal his heart, and her cookies always did the trick.

CHAPTER TEN

C oop had time for two cookies before Lois arrived. Gus opted to stay with AB, who was in the process of refilling his cookie jar. She often needed supervision during the procedure.

As Coop offered Lois a chair at the conference table, AB arrived with a tray of Camille's cookies and iced teas, leaving them on the end of the table before closing the door behind her.

Lois glanced at the tray. "I can't resist your aunt's cookies."

He laughed and took a glass of iced tea. "Me either."

"Thanks for stopping by. I didn't want to put you in a precarious position and talk at your office."

She nibbled on the edge of her cookie and shrugged. "I imagine it has to do with the audio of Randy and Michelle?"

He nodded. "Firestorm, right?"

"More like a nuclear weapon. I think Randy is going to resign his position. He's not happy and trying to blame

Michelle for her being dead isn't a good look. He's getting advice to step down."

"Do you think he knew about the audio release the night of the gala?"

She nodded. "Oh, yes. He mentioned it to me. Wanted me to intervene and talk some sense into Michelle."

Coop glanced at the diagram he'd made the night of the murder. "From my notes, I've got Randy, Marcus and his wife, a guy named Dylan from Marcus' office, Daniel Prescott from the governor's office, and another guy Brian, a staffer in the governor's office, at the same table, along with Mr. and Mrs. Winters. Is that what you remember?"

Her eyes squinted as she took a sip of iced tea. "Yeah, that sounds right. I walked by their table and remember them. Dylan is always with Marcus at events. Randy was working hard to assure Marcus he had the full support of the party, but at the same time, didn't want to alienate Emily Harper, who is very popular here in the Tennessee Senate. He was trying to keep both sides of his bread buttered."

Coop grimaced. "Randy sounds like the reason I have a low opinion of politicians." He caught himself and added, "Present company excluded."

She chuckled. "No offense taken. My family would like nothing more than for me to leave politics and fade back into obscurity when my term ends."

"I can only imagine." Coop studied the drawing. "Do you remember noticing if any of them left their table after dessert and the actors finished the murder scene?"

She sighed. "I'm not sure. Their table wasn't near ours, thanks to you choosing one so close to the patio. I'm trying to remember if I saw any of them when we were setting out for the library. I'm sorry, I don't know one way or the other."

Coop shrugged. "It was worth asking. This one is

tougher. Do you think any of them could have killed Michelle?"

Her eyes widened. "That's hard to say. Randy was furious. Beside himself. I'd never seen him in such a state. Marcus was his usual friendly self, but he was also bending my ear about needing my support to fend off both Michelle and Emily in a primary. I've always gotten along with him, but he's no ball of fire. He's where he is largely because of his father, who paved the way for him when he retired from Congress. I listened but didn't commit to anything. Honestly, Michelle or Emily would do a better job, but I wasn't saying that yet."

"What about Emily?"

She shook her head. "I don't see it. She's not underhanded. She and Michelle are both tough and have many of the same stances when it comes to policy. Emily is well-respected and liked by staff and colleagues. Her personality is opposite of Michelle's. She's more apt to work quietly and behind the scenes, only taking to the microphone or news outlets when it's important. Michelle was one who would always go for the jugular and come out swinging, sometimes before it was prudent."

"If you had to guess, which of the three would win the primary?"

"Tough to say since the money was behind the incumbent, but Emily also had a ton of support and some big PAC money. The people want action and change right now, so I think Marcus had a rough road ahead of him. Michelle had some big money behind her too, but I think she had a way of turning donors off with her brashness, so my money is on Emily."

He consulted his diagram of the tables at the gala. "Looks like Emily sat here." He pointed. "Jerry and Darlene

Anderson sat next to her. They sound familiar to me. Probably friends with Camille."

She nodded. "They're big donors of hers and great friends of Victoria and Arthur. Similar age bracket, and I'm sure Camille knows them. Both very kind and upstanding people."

Coop finished writing a note on his pad. "One more question. This one is more personal and delicate. During my investigations, a possible affair between Daniel Prescott and Michelle has come up. Have you heard rumblings or know anything?"

Lois' shoulders drooped. "I did hear rumors from Governor Brown himself. It was recent, and he was considering having a frank conversation with Daniel. Daniel is brilliant and a real star. The governor would be lost without him, but he didn't want anything to sully his office, and he planned to make it clear to Daniel that he needed to end it or risk his career. Governor Brown has been mentioned as a contender for a cabinet post, and he would take Daniel with him, but not if he's a liability."

Coop sat back in his chair. "Now, I need a huge favor."

Lois smiled. "I'll help you if I can."

———

To remove some people from the suspect column so Coop and AB could focus on those who had a true motive, Wednesday was packed with interviews of the guests at the gala.

Coop was able to eliminate the spousal counterparts at Michelle's table. They had been together and left the table in search of their clue. They both independently confirmed each other's alibis and had left in the direction of one of the living areas on the opposite side of the chateau.

By noon, he'd also been able to eliminate the real estate agents and their spouses, who had all been together searching the entry area for clues when Bridget joined them. He added his notes from those conversations to the large file.

The last appointment of the day was with Jonathan Winters, who was a mega donor to Michelle's campaigns and had set up a PAC for her run for Congress. He invited Coop to his home, so after dropping Gus off with his dad and Aunt Camille and changing into a button down with a sports jacket, Coop drove a mile down the road to the neighborhood close to the park where Gus loved to play. He drove the Jeep through the massive gate and to the Winters' huge mansion that reminded Coop of something he would see in the French countryside.

Along with Aunt Camille's knowledge, AB's background report on Mr. Winters showcased his success in the financial and wealth management sector. He was well respected and had many A-list clients in the music industry in Nashville.

Coop parked in the sweeping driveway and took the stone and brick pathway to the front door. Before he could knock, a gray-haired man, dressed in an impeccable suit, greeted him. "Mr. Harrington," he said, extending his hand. "Welcome and please come in."

Suddenly glad he'd listened to AB and worn the sports jacket, Coop shook his hand. "Thanks for seeing me, Mr. Winters." Coop followed him through the impressive home to a huge porch overlooking the vast backyard and trees that circled the perimeter of the acreage.

"Call me John, please." As soon as they sat on the white upholstered chairs with a view of the brick patio and the fountain, a woman appeared with a tray of lemonade, iced tea, and bottles of cold beer and left them on the coffee table, exiting as quickly as she arrived.

At John's encouragement, Coop helped himself to a tall glass of iced tea, secretly wishing he wasn't driving so he could indulge in a cold beer. He would have walked had he known.

Coop found that John's voice, with its soft drawl, reminded him of his uncle. "Victoria tells me you're to be trusted and that you're looking into that ghastly business at the gala for them." John took a long swallow from the beer he'd chosen.

"Yes, sir. I'm doing my best to get a feel for those close to Michelle and who might have killed her. The Sinclairs are quite upset."

"Oh, I can imagine. Victoria and Arthur are both pillars of the community, and I understand their need to get this solved quickly. As you probably know, I was a financial backer of Michelle's. I had been since her first foray into politics in the Tennessee Assembly."

"Did you talk to Michelle that night? Did you witness anything that would give you pause regarding her death?"

"I only said hello to her in passing. I did mention that we should talk this week. I was concerned about the audio she had leaked with Randy Boone." His jaw tightened. "I wasn't sure it was a wise move. I understood it, of course. Michelle enjoyed the shock and awe that brought her attention."

"You were seated with Mr. Boone that night."

He nodded. "Yes, I've always been a big supporter of the party. Randy was trying to convince me to dump Michelle and put my resources behind Marcus."

"Was he convincing?"

Mr. Winters chuckled. "I've learned not to comment or commit to anything too quickly. I keep my own counsel. I listened, of course, but wasn't about to abandon Michelle based on Randy's advice. Randy is an opportunist. A political weathervane, some might say. I thought Michelle was a strong candidate, but I'm not naïve and when it comes to politics, I'm more concerned about our party winning. If Michelle's tactic didn't work, or she stepped away, I most likely would put my backing with Emily. She's a worker with strong principles."

"How upset was Randy about the audio leak?"

His eyes widened. "Oh, he was furious. Spittin' mad and working overtime to convince everyone Michelle was the villain and she needed to go down in flames for her betrayal."

"Do you think he's capable of murder?"

He stared at the fountain for a few moments. "I think under the right circumstances, we're all capable of murder. That night, he was angrier than I've ever seen him. I don't know that he would kill Michelle, but he definitely wanted her erased from the ticket and the party."

"Do you remember him or anyone from your table leaving after the actors performed the murder scene when the lights flickered?"

The creases in his forehead deepened. "Well, my wife Jolene went to the ladies room, and I seem to remember Daniel also excused himself right as she did." He stared outside and then turned his head back to Coop. "Randy left, and Marcus followed. I don't know where they went."

"Was anyone at your table playing the murder mystery game?"

He shook his head. "No, everyone at our table was focused on the impending political wildfire Michelle had sparked. All of them were bent over their phones, texting or checking online. Jolene and I planned to make an early escape home. I'd heard enough of the teeth gnashing. Randy's constant whining and groveling to Marcus was growing loathsome."

"You mentioned Emily Harper. It sounds like she was a solid rival to Michelle and Marcus?"

He nodded. "Oh, yes, she certainly is. I supported Emily in her run for senator. She's done good work, stood by her promises and principles. I would have preferred Michelle run for Emily's seat here in the Tennessee Senate instead of Congress, but Michelle wasn't one to wait her turn." He laughed. "I admired that about her, but she tended to jump in with both feet to buck the system without giving it the thought it sometimes deserved. I planned to discuss that with her this week. She waited until the filing deadline on Thursday to put her name on the primary ticket and then unleashed that damning audio Friday night."

"I've heard Randy is getting pressured to resign."

He took a long swallow from his beer. "Yes, I think that's for the best. He's put a stain on himself and the party. He's a liability now, and candidates and donors want nothing to do with him, not to mention those in power at a higher level." He paused and added, "He was an idiot to do what he did, but Michelle effectively ruined his career. At least here in Tennessee and quite possibly beyond our borders."

"Do you think Marcus or Daniel would have a reason to want Michelle dead?"

"She was a definite thorn in Marcus' side. A real threat, as was Emily. Emily was more refined and didn't make big moves. Michelle was unpredictable and was already capitalizing on the thirst the people of Tennessee had for accountability. They, along with the whole country, are tired of politicians promising one thing and never delivering. Michelle was striking a deep chord with those grassroots who wanted new blood in Washington."

Coop scribbled in his notebook and was about to close it when a woman, dressed in an expensive pantsuit and pearls, came into the room. She smiled at Coop as John stood and reached for her hand. "Darling, this is Mr. Harrington. He's investigating the ugly business with Michelle at the gala."

Coop stood and extended his hand. "Mrs. Winters, lovely to meet you."

"You're Camille's nephew, right?"

"Yes, ma'am."

"I've known her forever." She pointed at Coop's chair. "Don't leave on my account. I was just popping in to let John know dinner will be about an hour. I just got home."

John pointed to the end of the couch next to his chair. "Sit down, darling. I think Mr. Harrington would like to ask you a few questions about that evening at Victoria's."

She helped herself to a glass of iced tea and sat on the edge of the couch. "I'm happy to help."

Coop ask her for her observations, and she admitted that she tuned out the political talk at their table and did a bit of people watching, enjoying all the fancy gowns the women wore at the gala. She confirmed that she did use the ladies room after the murder scene.

"Which bathroom did you use? I think Victoria told me there are six on the ground level."

She grinned. "Most of them are ensuites, but she's got two in that hallway near the library and music room. One at each end of it. I visited the furthest one as the first one closest to the library was in use. There's also a powder room off the patio near the kitchen, and I think another powder room near the entryway. The other two bathrooms are connected to the bedrooms in that wing that shoots off to the formal living area."

Coop made a note as she spoke. "Sounds like you've been there before?"

"Oh, heavens yes, many times. Victoria and Arthur have always been generous with their home for fundraising and charity events, and we're personal friends."

"Did you see anyone in the hallway on your way to the restroom or when you returned to the table? Or coming from the library?"

She cocked her head. "Now that you mention it, I did see Daniel on my way to use the restroom. It looked like he was coming from the vicinity of the library."

"Anybody else?"

"There was a young woman waiting to use the restroom when I came out. I didn't pay close attention and didn't recognize her. She had a beautiful blue gown. There were people milling about who were intent on finding the clues for the game."

Coop nodded and closed his notebook. "I appreciate your help. If either of you think of anything, please reach out to me. Even if it seems insignificant. The smallest details often unlock a case like this."

Mr. Winters rose and walked Coop to the door. "Best of luck, Mr. Harrington. If we can be of help, don't hesitate to call on us again."

Coop thanked him and slipped behind the wheel of his Jeep. With Mrs. Winters' revelation about Daniel, tomorrow's meetings were even more important.

CHAPTER ELEVEN

As she promised, Lois came through and introduced Coop to Emily, Daniel, and Randy. She'd also arranged a video call with Marcus, who was back in D.C. He could fit Coop in first thing Thursday morning. While Coop waited for the telltale chime from his computer, he took a long sip of strong coffee from his cup.

AB sat in a chair at the edge of Coop's desk, off camera, so she could observe and note anything of substance. Bored with the whole early morning rush after his breakfast, Gus rested in the leather chair in the corner, his eyes barely able to stay open.

After five minutes of waiting, the sound for the video call came through, and Coop connected. Marcus appeared, his dark hair perfectly styled, his pinstripe suit and matching pocket square and tie, impeccable. Coop was sure his handsome features were part of the reason he was in Congress. "Mr. Harrington. As I told Speaker Evans, I hope you understand that my availability is limited, and I can only offer you a few minutes of my very valuable time."

Marcus turned his head away from the camera. "Dylan, where is my latte? And where are the lemon slices for my water?" He shook his head with an air of disgust and turned back to the camera.

His superior attitude and tone annoyed Coop, but he held his tongue. He longed to remind him that a murder investigation often required more than a few minutes and wanted nothing more than to make it clear to Marcus that he wasn't his employee or underling. Marcus worked for him and all the good people of Tennessee. This clown was the epitome of what was wrong with politicians today.

Instead, Coop took a breath and launched into his questioning. "Well then, since time is short, let's cut to the chase. Did you murder, arrange for the murder, or know who murdered Michelle Roberts?"

The look of horror on Marcus' face was priceless. His mouth was agape, and it took a few moments for the polished legislator to restore his smile and demeanor that graced the flyers and mailers he sent by the thousands to constituents.

Coop took in the scene while a hand behind Marcus delivered a bowl of lemon slices and then a latte from a well-known coffee chain.

Marcus' fake smile couldn't hide the contempt in his voice. "I most certainly did not murder Michelle, nor do I know anything about who might have done it. I take great offense to you suggesting I do."

Coop grinned. "It wasn't a suggestion. It was a question, and you're the one who gave me only a few minutes, which means I have to prioritize my queries. I have a few more for you. Congressman, you were absent from the table at the gala during the time of Michelle's murder. Where did you go after the actors completed the murder scene for the game?"

His high forehead wrinkled. "I was on the phone off and on throughout the evening. I'm just trying to remember."

After a few moments, Marcus looked into the camera. "I remember now. Randy wanted to talk to me in private, and we slipped into the music room for a few minutes. We weren't there long, then I used the restroom in the hallway."

"Who left the music room first?"

"Uh, Randy left. I was checking something on my phone and then went to the restroom."

"Which restroom? There are two of them."

"Uh, the one at the end of the hallway just down from the music room."

"Michelle getting in the primary was a threat to you, was it not?"

Marcus responded with a patronizing chuckle. "I wouldn't say a threat. More of a nuisance. Part of what Randy wanted to tell me was that the party was supporting me."

"You trusted Randy, even after the whole mess with the audio Michelle released of him offering her a bribe?"

He waved his hand. "I'd heard rumblings of it on Saturday, but none of the mainstream media was interested. It's more fodder for the conspiracy wing of our party."

"So, you didn't take it seriously then? What about now that it's being reported and discussed across all the news outlets? I have it on pretty good authority that Randy is resigning. Were you the muscle behind his offer to pay Michelle off if she'd step away from her run for your seat?"

A vivid flush rose from the collar of Marcus' white shirt, and his cheeks turned a rosy shade of crimson that matched his silk tie. Any hint of friendliness disappeared from his tone. "I had nothing to do with what Randy did. I think it's best for the party if he does step down, and I told him that yesterday."

"Can you speculate who might have been behind the offer Randy was making?"

Marcus shrugged. "No idea. Maybe another candidate. Maybe Emily?"

"You haven't heard any rumblings in D.C. about it? People nervous that they might be found out to be behind the bribe? You really expect me or anyone else to believe Randy took it upon himself to offer an almost unlimited amount of money or a prestigious position without the backing of someone?"

The smile, fake or otherwise, was gone. Through clenched jaws, Marcus spat out a reply, "As I said, I have no idea or knowledge of where the offer came from. Randy would be the one to ask."

Coop was enjoying this. It was like being in the courtroom and questioning a hostile witness. One who thought he was smarter than everyone in the room. "Did you see anyone else when you were on your way to and from the music room and the restroom in the hallway? Notice anyone coming or going near the library?"

The change in the line of questioning caught Marcus off guard. He was all teed up for another question about Randy. "I, uh, well, let me think." After a moment, he said, "I think Mrs. Winters was in the hallway. Randy of course. He was already in the music room by the time I arrived. I think Daniel was also there, maybe looking for the restroom. I'm not sure."

"Anyone else? Your staff? Your wife? Did Dylan leave the table or go with you?"

He shook his head. "No, Randy was insistent that we meet alone, and Dylan stayed behind at the table. My wife was still working on her dessert."

Marcus glanced over at someone off camera. "I'll be right there. Thanks, Dylan."

"Dylan is on my list to interview. Let him know I'll be in touch today. It looks like you're needed for that very important meeting you mentioned, and I'm due to talk with the chief of detectives here in Nashville. Thanks so much for your time, Congressman. It's been enlightening."

Marcus held up his hand. "Wait, uh, if you have more questions, I can make myself available. I'm sorry it's such a rush this morning."

"Not a problem. As I said, I've got another appointment myself. Appreciate your offer." Coop signed off and disconnected the call.

Coop could always gauge AB's level of concern by the height of her arched brows. When he turned to look at her, they were higher than he ever remembered.

"Wow," was all she said.

"Is that a good wow or a bad wow?"

She laughed. "He pushed a button, obviously."

Coop grimaced with disgust and shook his head. "He's a pompous snob. You know how much I hate being around politicians. He's the prime example of why. Demanding lemons and lattes, like a little emperor. I've said it before, and I'll say it again, we'd be better off picking five hundred and thirty-five people from the phone book to represent us than being stuck with the likes of Marcus. Even his name is smarmy."

"Your distrust of politicians aside, what do you think?"

With a shrug, Coop grunted. "He has a motive and the opportunity since he was in the area of the murder during the small window of time. I'm not sure about the means. Yet."

Coop tapped the notepad with his pen. "I doubt he would dirty his hands himself. He strikes me more as someone capable of pulling strings behind the scenes and having someone do it. That begs the question of who would he have do it?"

"His staff was there, but that seems like a pretty big ask."

Coop nodded. "And too close to connect him. It would be someone not so easily connected to him." He studied the guest list and the seating chart.

"Eliza Dugan, Michelle's attorney, is coming in this morning on her way to work. You're set up to video chat with Dylan at ten o'clock. Maybe he'll shed some light on things. I have a call into Marcus' wife, too."

"How are we doing on getting a time set up for Daniel and Randy?"

AB checked her notes. "I'm waiting for a return call from Randy but haven't been able to talk to anyone. I've just left several messages and made sure he knew we were the people Lois had talked to him about." She took a sip from her cup. "Daniel is supposed to let me know today, as is his staffer who was in attendance, Brian."

Coop's eyes narrowed. "I'm going to call Mr. Winters and see if he can light a fire under Randy. We need to get to him before he resigns and turns off his phone or leaves town."

AB nodded. "I've got his home address, so if that doesn't work, a surprise visit might."

With a mischievous grin, Coop caught AB's eye. "That's why you're my favorite, AB." He tapped his temple. "We think alike."

Eliza Dugan arrived just after eight o'clock. She was in and out of Coop's office within thirty minutes. While he waited for his scheduled video calls with Marcus' staffer, Coop filled his cup with decaf, grabbed two cookies from the box on the counter, and parked himself next to AB's desk, where he offered her one of the cookies.

As soon as he bit into his cookie, Mrs. Ryle called into the office and as much as Coop would have rather had her on a video call, he didn't expect to learn much from her and interviewed her via telephone.

She was cordial but had nothing to add of any substance. She didn't leave the table and had no idea what time her husband left or returned. Coop took the call in the reception area with AB listening.

As soon as he disconnected, AB cocked her head. "She was a waste of time." She gestured toward the door. "What did you learn from Michelle's lawyer?"

"Not much I didn't already know. She didn't leave the table and was never in the hallway by the library, so she had nothing to offer as far as observing anyone. She also indicated that she had advised Michelle against releasing the audio. Sounds like Michelle was determined to take Randy down. She had some strong negative feelings about him and his failure to help support all the candidates in the primary. Michelle was intent on ousting the good old boys and wanted to shake things up. Eliza also confirmed that Michelle made generous provisions for her daughter in her will, but the bulk of everything went to her husband Joe, including a million-dollar life insurance policy. He'll get their house, investments, accounts, and her share of Zen." Coop's forehead wrinkled. "Well, provided Mr. Carlisle signs her shares over to him. That could get sticky."

"A million bucks is some strong motive. I doubt Mr. Carlisle will give Joe controlling interest, based on his lack of skill as a businessman. That will be interesting." AB checked her watch. "I plan to visit Zen this week and see if I can get a read on Joe or Paula. I called the Franklin location to see if Joe was in, and they told me he's at Green Hills all week, getting ready for the celebration of life. Might be fun to pop in and see what I can learn by observing them. When I called, I spoke with Paula, and she said I could stop by for a tour anytime."

He nodded. "Good idea. I left Joe a message on Tuesday, I think it was, but haven't heard back. I'll call him and set up a time to interview him. We'll make sure you're not present, so he doesn't recognize you."

After his cookie break, Coop went back to his office and studied the list of guests and his smaller suspect column. Randy, Marcus, and Daniel all stood out based on their location and possible motives. Emily was also on the list and was on the schedule for later this evening. Sometimes there weren't enough hours in the day.

By noon, Coop finished with his other video call to Washington, D.C. He followed AB out of his office and slumped onto the couch by her desk. "So, you agree Dylan wasn't much help?"

She nodded. "He parroted what Marcus said earlier." She checked her notes. "He was at the table during the time the others were gone. Spent all his time on his phone, checking social media, legislative email, constituent email, and polls. He didn't know Michelle personally, only by reputation. He wasn't a fan of hers, but I didn't get the impression it went beyond being on an adversarial team."

"You caught that mention of polls, too. Dylan tried to gloss over his little mistake, since technically as an employee of the government, he shouldn't be involved in any campaign activities. He tried to cover it by saying it was legislative polls. I'm sure it was Marcus' campaign polls."

"Bottom line," said AB with a sigh, "I don't think he was

involved in Michelle's murder. He never left the table and didn't know much beyond Marcus' talking points of Michelle being too inexperienced and naïve to navigate the complicated legislative process in D.C."

Coop welcomed Gus next to him and petted his ears. "I did think it was telling when Dylan mentioned how popular Emily was, and he thought she was the biggest threat to Marcus."

"And Marcus made a point of trying to suggest Emily might be behind the bribery scheme Randy tried to sell Michelle."

Coop nodded as he stroked the fur on Gus' back. "I can't keep thinking of that old joke about knowing when a politician is lying."

AB laughed. "When his lips are moving."

"Exactly. So, were Marcus and his team more worried about Emily or Michelle? Could he have orchestrated Michelle's demise and implicated Emily at the same time?"

"That eliminates both threats." AB's forehead wrinkled. "I don't know."

"Me either," said Coop. "Part of me thinks he'd do anything to keep his position, but the other part of me thinks he's too lazy to come up with something like that. Victoria divulged that they thought Marcus was more talk than walk. I got that same impression from our call today."

CHAPTER TWELVE

Coop hung up the phone from a call with Randy, who stressed how busy he was and how he didn't have much time to meet. Coop was firm in his request, dropped Victoria's name, along with Mr. Winters, and by the end of the chat, he had an appointment with Randy tonight. Randy requested to meet at his home, worried about prying eyes watching him at his own office.

With no hope of dinner between meeting with Emily and his new appointment with Randy, Coop nibbled on another cookie. As he finished it, he gazed out his office window and noticed a sleek BMW pull to the curb. Daniel arrived right on time. Coop watched as he emerged from his car, straightened his tie, and made his way up the sidewalk.

Coop brushed the crumbs from his shirt, gave Gus a quick pat on the head, and stationed himself behind his desk. Minutes later, AB led him back to Coop's office. AB mentioned something about him being the area's most eligible bachelor and as Coop took in his handsomeness, he understood why. He was what most women would call a catch. Nice hair, million-dollar smile, athletic build, cool car, and a high-profile job. What more could they want?

Coop extended his hand. "Mr. Prescott, thanks so much for taking the time to come here today. We appreciate it."

His visitor smiled and said, "Call me Daniel, please." When he noticed Gus' tail thumping against the leather seat of his chair, he grinned at him.

Coop caught a whiff of Daniel's aftershave and remembered the scent. He'd smelled it before when they'd all walked into the library at the gala on their hunt for clues. It was a distinctive and rather heavy scent.

AB offered Daniel something to drink, and he opted for sweet tea. Another point in his favor.

Coop sat behind his desk and motioned Daniel to an empty chair in front of it. "Have a seat, and we'll get right to it. I'm sure you have things to do."

As he sat, AB arrived with a tray of tea and cookies and left them on the edge of the desk before taking the chair next to Daniel, where her notepad waited.

"As I'm sure Speaker Evans explained, we've been retained by the Sinclairs to look into Ms. Roberts' murder that occurred at their home during the recent gala you attended. We're trying to get a clear picture of where people were during the incident and record your observations about the evening. At this point, we know you sat with several others, and you and some of them left the table after the actors completed their murder scene during the dessert portion of the evening. Is that correct?"

Daniel nodded and reached for his glass of tea. "That's right. Randy wanted to talk to Marcus, so they wandered off together. I needed to use the restroom and left as soon as the scene finished."

"Which restroom did you use?"

"Uh, the one in the hallway, closest to the big hall where we had dinner." He gulped down another swallow of iced tea. Coop nodded. "Did you go into the library before or after you used the restroom?"

Daniel coughed and choked. He reached for a napkin and wiped his mouth. "Sorry, uh, the library?"

"That's right." The familiar scent of Daniel's cologne gave Coop the nudge to stretch the facts. "You were seen coming from the library, where Michelle was found dead. We're just trying to narrow down the timing."

He sighed. "I used the restroom and when I came out, I saw Michelle through the glass door of the library. She tapped on the door and motioned me to join her."

"What was the nature of your conversation with her?"

"She was looking at the mockup of her campaign website and wanted my opinion."

"So, you two were close?"

"Uh, well..." He reached for his iced tea again. After a long swallow, he darted his eyes toward AB and then back at Coop.

"If it makes things easier, we're aware that you and Ms. Roberts were involved in a personal relationship." Coop raised his brows at Daniel.

As Coop spoke, Daniel's shoulders lowered, and he sat back in his chair. He hung his head for a few moments and then met Coop's eyes. "I'm ashamed to admit it, but yes, Michelle and I were romantically involved. I told her last week that I couldn't continue the relationship."

"How did that go over?" asked Coop.

Daniel shrugged. "I think she knew it had run its course. It wasn't a wise move for either of us. We got carried away."

Coop's forehead creased. "So, if you two agreed you were

done with your affair, why would she invite you to join her in the library at the gala?"

"She was excited about her website and wanted my opinion. That's how all of this started. We got close talking policy and strategy, and it just morphed into an intimate relationship."

"How long were you in the library with her?"

"Only a few minutes. She had the site up on her phone, and I gave her a couple of small ideas for improvement. I wasn't comfortable being there with her alone after we agreed to stop seeing each other."

"Where was she in the library?"

"She was sitting in a chair. There were two chairs separated by a little velvet sofa."

"Just for the record, did you do anything to harm her while you were in the library? What was her condition when you left? And would you say you were there for five minutes or how long?"

He shook his head. "I did nothing to her. I chatted for a few minutes and was anxious to leave. I would guess no more than five minutes, probably less. I wanted to avoid any perception of impropriety, and the last thing I needed was a rumor getting back to the office about me and Michelle. When I left, she was in the chair, looking at her phone."

"We've heard Governor Brown may be tapped for a cabinet position, and he made it clear that he didn't approve of your affair with Michelle and wouldn't be taking you with him if it continued. Is that accurate?"

Shame replaced the light in Daniel's eyes. He nodded slowly. "I'd say that sums it up. As I said, I know it was wrong and a total lapse in judgment. The decision to break off the relationship was an easy one. We both knew it wasn't a forever deal. I wasn't upset and understood where the governor was coming from. He was right. I think Michelle's ego may have been wounded, but we didn't speak of it that night. In my mind, it was forgotten, and I would never do anything to harm her or anyone else."

Coop nodded. "Did you see anyone else approach the library or see anyone else in that hallway when you were coming or going?"

"There was nobody around when I went into the library. I looked to make sure the coast was clear when I left, but I remember seeing Marcus and Randy in the hall. Oh, and Emily Harper was there, too. I remember saying hello to her."

"So, you went back to the table after leaving the library?"

"Right." He nodded.

"Do you know what time that was?"

He shrugged, then his eyes widened. He dug his phone out of his pocket. "I replied to an email when I sat. Let me check." He tapped his screen and then nodded. "Here it is. My reply was at 8:21."

Coop added a note to his tablet. "What's your theory on who murdered Michelle?"

He shook his head. "I can't really fathom the idea of someone killing her?"

"From what we've learned, she wasn't known for winning friends in the political arena. Seems like she ruffled quite a few feathers. Most recently, those of Randy Boone. Did she ever talk about anyone threatening her?"

"She never mentioned threats. All politicians get weird letters and emails from people who are angry at their policies or whatever, but Michelle never worried about them. As far as Randy goes, Michelle was almost giddy after she released that audio. She had a big smile when I mentioned it that night at the gala. She knew he was upset, but she didn't care. Didn't seem worried in the least."

"Do you think Marcus or Emily were threatened enough by her to take steps to kill her?"

Daniel's eyes widened again. "I think that's a step too far. I know they both wanted to win the seat, as did Michelle, but I really don't see either of them making such a crazy move. Marcus was convinced he would retain the seat. At least outwardly, he never expressed concern about her. I've never heard Emily say anything derogatory about Michelle."

"What about Randy?"

Daniel's jaw twitched. "He was mad. Beyond mad. I've known him for years and can't remember seeing him so angry. I can't imagine him killing her, but he was furious and worried about his job."

Coop finished adding a note. "You're not married, but do you have a serious girlfriend? Anyone who would be jealous of your relationship with Michelle?"

He laughed. "Not married, no serious girlfriend. I'm married to my job. Nobody to get jealous."

"What about Michelle's husband Joe?"

"Only met him a couple of times. At political events. Michelle never said much about him. We didn't have that kind of relationship. We didn't talk about our lives. It was all centered on our work in politics."

"How often did you, uh, see one another romantically?" Coop asked.

With a long sigh, Daniel shrugged. "Maybe once a week or so. It was all spontaneous. We didn't meet up for dinner dates."

"And these meetings took place where?"

"Usually at Michelle's office. Once or twice at a hotel when we were both attending events out of town."

"Never at your office or home?"

"No. I was dumb to get involved, but I'm not a big enough idiot to entertain Michelle in the governor's office. As I said, I knew it was wrong. She had a big personality and was hard to resist."

"So, Michelle was the main instigator in the relationship?"

"Yeah, she approached me the first time. I should have said no, but I didn't."

"And as far as you know, her husband didn't know about the affair?"

"Right. I never got that impression, and Michelle wasn't worried about it." He took another drink of tea. "It was entertainment. Letting off steam. Nothing more, really."

"One more question," said Coop. "Does knowing Michelle was killed with a lethal dose of succinylcholine bring to mind anyone who might have access to that drug and be willing to commit murder with it?"

Daniel frowned. "I don't know much about that drug. I guess someone in the medical field would be most likely, but nobody comes to mind." He stammered and then added, "Randy's wife Elana was a doctor, but I'm not sure exactly what kind. I don't think she practices any longer. She's a professor now."

After scribbling on his notepad, Coop looked across the desk. "Thanks, Daniel. That's helpful. If you think of anything else or someone comes to mind that you think might be involved in the murder, please call me." He handed him a business card.

Daniel nodded at AB and shook Coop's hand. "Thank you. I'm truly sorry about her. She was a good person. Driven, for sure, and often harsh in her approach, but her heart was in the right place. I'll be sure to reach out if I think of anything that might help."

He started for the door, and Coop followed him out to the reception area.

As Daniel stepped out of the office, he turned. "I appreciate you meeting me here and not creating a scene for me at work."

"No problem," said Coop. "I'm not here to judge your personal life. Only to dig as far as necessary to find the person who murdered Ms. Roberts."

With a sad look, Daniel nodded. "I hope you find him, Mr. Harrington. I really do."

CHAPTER THIRTEEN

C oop left AB to shut down the office for the evening and dropped Gus with his dad and Camille before he continued to Emily's house. She lived in Franklin, about thirty minutes from Coop's domain.

He made his way to the large gate hung between thick stone pillars that made up the fencing surrounding the acreage. He pressed the intercom button, and the gate swung open. The long driveway that ran through green fields led to a house tucked into the trees.

Coop parked the Jeep and followed the stone walkway to the front door of the dark-wood structure. The angular style of it reminded Coop of homes popular in the 1970s. He waited at the door of the split-level home for a few moments before a blond woman he recognized as Emily Harper opened it. She welcomed him inside with a warm smile.

"Come on in and have a seat in the living room." She led him to an open room on the main level with a floor-to-ceiling stone fireplace and oversized leather couches. "Can I get you anything to drink?"

Coop held up his hand. "No, thank you. I appreciate you seeing me and don't want to take up more time than necessary."

"Lois speaks very highly of you." She took a seat on the couch and motioned to the other one adjacent to it for him.

"She's been very helpful getting me access to people who were at the gala the night Michelle Roberts was murdered."

She shook her head. "It's truly horrific. While we differed in style and approach, Michelle and I shared many of the same underlying policy beliefs."

"As you probably know, Michelle was killed in the library. I've been interviewing guests to determine their whereabouts during the incident. From talking with others, you were in the area of the library, in that main hallway."

She nodded. "Yes, I visited the restroom. I rushed to it in fact, while the actors told people to check their envelopes for directions. I wanted to beat the rush."

"Did you see Ms. Roberts or go into the library while you were there?"

Emily shook her head. "No, I didn't see Michelle there. I saw her earlier in the evening when I was roaming around the room before I took my seat. I never saw her again."

"Did you notice anyone go into the library or see others in that area?"

She sighed. "I remember seeing Marcus and Randy when I came from the restroom. Neither of them was overly friendly when I said hello. They seemed to be on a mission and were moving quickly down the hallway. Daniel from Governor Brown's office was there. I saw him heading toward the restroom as I left the hallway. I'm not sure where he was coming from, as I didn't really take notice. There were quite a few people milling about with some playing the game and searching for clues."

Coop nodded. "Did you talk with Randy about the audio Michelle leaked?"

Her eyes widened. "We talked for a few minutes before dinner. He was doing his best to salvage his reputation and assured me it was taken out of context." She shook her head. "I know his loyalty was to Marcus. He wasn't sure how things would play out, so he didn't want to alienate me, just in case I won. He'd been supportive of me in the past. He was sort of stuck between a rock and a hard place, but it wasn't lost on me that he was aligned with Marcus."

"Did you consider Michelle a threat in the primary?"

She nodded. "Sure. We share many of the same constituency, so I'd be foolish not to take her seriously. Part of what Randy told me when we chatted was that he urged Michelle to run for my seat here in Tennessee, where she would win easily, without much effort. He thought she'd have a better chance if she waited her turn to run after serving in the Tennessee Senate."

"Did you ask him to do that or encourage Michelle to get out of the race and try for your seat here?"

She shook her head. "No, I didn't discuss it with her or with Randy. My campaign manager did reach out to her people and suggest that and shared that we'd support her in her run for my Senate seat. Michelle didn't ask me for counsel and although I'd heard inklings of her throwing her hat into the run for US Congress, she didn't make it official until the very last day to file. Part of me hoped she wouldn't, of course, since we'd be splitting votes between us, so it could have very easily swung the election for Marcus."

With a quick shrug of her shoulders, she added, "But I know Michelle, and she's not one to go along to get along. She likes the shock factor and isn't one to sit and wait her turn."

Coop's forehead creased. "So, without Michelle in the race, your chances of beating Marcus greatly increase?"

Emily's smile faltered as her jaw tensed. "Yes, it does, but that doesn't mean I was involved in her murder. I would never resort to such tactics. I think I'm the best person for the job, but no job is worth selling my soul. I have a strong belief in the voters being smart enough to see the differences in candidates and was banking on my relationships with them, the voters, not the elites in the party, to give me the job. I believe in our system of government and was determined to give it my all on the campaign trail and prove to the voters that I'm the best person to be their representative."

"A novel approach in this age of big money and the corruption so many of us feel drives politics."

She nodded. "It's changed so much over my career. I think I could make a difference in Washington, which is why I decided to run. I'm also not naïve and understand I don't have the same support Marcus does. I've served in the Tennessee Assembly and the Senate and if I lose this race, I'm happy to go back to spending time here at home and with my husband."

"He's in the music industry, right?"

She smiled. "Yeah, he's in a band and on the road quite a bit, like he is tonight. If I lose, I'd have the freedom to travel with him more and maybe pursue new interests. Our daughter is also expecting a baby, so I'd have more time to be a grandma. I have a life in politics, but it's not my entire life, so I'm good either way."

"Going back to the gala. You used the restroom and then went back to your table?"

She nodded and then stopped herself. "I went over to the

bar first. I needed another sweet tea. I make it a point not to drink alcohol at public events."

"Any idea what time that was?"

She sighed. "I had time enough to get back to my table and drink about half my glass before Victoria made the announcement to get everyone back to their tables due to a medical emergency." Her forehead creased, and she gasped. "Wait, wait. I actually got a text from my husband and answered it while I was at the bar waiting for my drink."

Emily hurried from her seat and returned with her cell phone. She tapped the screen several times and then turned the phone to Coop. "I answered the text at 8:19."

Coop scribbled the time down on his notepad. "Thanks, that's very helpful. With so many guests, it's really quite a job to narrow down where people were during the murder."

She set her phone on the end table next to the couch. "I can only imagine."

Coop closed his notebook. "Not sure if you've heard, but Michelle was killed with a lethal dose of succinylcholine, a drug used in surgical procedures. Any ideas who would be willing to kill Michelle that might have access to that?"

Her lips flattened as she shook her head. "I'd heard rumors that it was a strange drug. There were several people in attendance affiliated with the medical industry, which is so large with Vanderbilt being here. I can see why I'd be at the top of the list, since Michelle's death, as you said will make my campaign easier, so I would imagine Marcus is on that same list."

She bit her bottom lip. "I'm no fan of his but can't imagine he'd take such a drastic step. Randy was beside himself and quite worried about the audio and wasn't a fan of Michelle. Again, it's hard to imagine him killing her, though. Michelle wasn't one to make friends in the political arena, so I'm sure there are others who didn't care for her. I don't know much about her personal life; she has a bit of a reputation when it comes to wandering from her marriage vows."

"Had you heard anything recent about affairs she might have been having or anything of that nature?"

Emily's nose wrinkled. "There's always scuttlebutt among those at the Capitol Complex, especially staffers. Michelle was very handsy when it came to hugging people and touching them. It left her open for gossip and innuendo when it came to men. I don't know of anything credible and only heard that Daniel from Governor Brown's office had been seen coming from Michelle's office after hours. That in itself is not an indictment. In her position, she works very closely with the governor's staff. Daniel is also a handsome single guy, who draws the attention of female staffers. It could all be innocent. Michelle didn't care much what people thought, so it may not have occurred to her that her decision to have those types of meetings after hours gives fodder to those looking for scandals. In a nutshell, that's what sets us apart. I've got a better sense of judgment and give things thought where she was more spontaneous and almost took delight in shocking people. She didn't mind negative attention."

Coop rose from his seat. "I appreciate your time." He handed her a business card. "If you do think of anything else you remember from that night or someone else I should talk to, please get in touch."

She smiled and followed him to the front door. "I'll do that. Thanks for taking time out of your evening to come all the way out here."

Coop thanked her again and made his way to the Jeep. Her timeline would help him whittle down those who had the opportunity to slip into the library and kill Michelle in what was becoming a very small window.

———

Coop slid into the driver's seat and pulled out his cell phone, which had vibrated while he was talking with Emily. He tapped the message from AB. She summarized the background she'd been able to pull together on Randy's wife Elana. She had been a surgeon and left medicine to teach at Vanderbilt. She wasn't full time and split her time between Nashville and Washington, D.C. She was teaching during the current semester and wouldn't be off until the summer break.

Elana was a clinical professor and trained students in a hospital setting. AB made it clear she would have access to drugs like succinylcholine.

Coop replied with his typical thumbs up emoji and hurried down the driveway. He left Franklin and made his way back to Forest Hills. Traffic was light and within twenty minutes, he pulled to the curb in front of Randy's house. Coop followed the brick-lined pathway to the small porch area of a single-story, ranch-style home.

He rang the bell and waited at the oversized wooden and glass-paned door, where a festive wreath hung. After several moments, Randy opened the door.

Coop took in the harried look on his face and extended his hand. "Thanks for seeing me, Mr. Boone."

Randy shook his hand and motioned him inside, darting his head out the door to look left and right.

"Come on in through here." Randy led Coop through the short entryway and into the living space open to the kitchen.

Coop took one of the chairs, and Randy selected the one

on the other side of the room. "I'm in a bit of a hurry as I'm sure you understand."

Coop nodded and slipped his notebook from his pocket. "I'm trying to determine where you were when Michelle was murdered. Did you encounter Michelle after the actors finished the murder scene? Did you visit the library at any time?"

Randy's eyes widened. "Marcus and I left the table, as did Mrs. Winters, I recall." He thought for a moment and added, "I remember seeing Emily Harper in the hallway when Marcus and I were on our way to the music room."

"Why did you and Marcus leave the table?"

He sighed. "I was trying to assure him that he could count on me and the party to continue to support him. With Michelle releasing that audio, I wanted to make sure Marcus knew I was focused on him. I was fighting for my reputation, and he has lots of sway with the party. He was upset because in the audio, I had alluded to being the messenger for others wanting Michelle out of the race. He thought I'd implicated him."

"Was he behind the request?"

Randy's face went pale, and he looked like he was going to vomit. "There are factions in the party within the House of Representatives that thought it best Michelle didn't run. They wanted to keep Marcus in his position."

"Were you asked to deliver the same message to Emily Harper?"

He shook his head. "No. Emily was formidable, but Michelle was openly talking about corruption and intimating the audio release was the tip of the iceberg. She supposedly had proof of kickbacks and other things that would bring into question the leadership of our party in Congress and Marcus. She was intent on shining the light on important people, far more than just Marcus. When I encouraged her to drop out, it was to help her. To warn her."

Coop frowned. "What do you mean warn her?"

He sighed and lowered his voice. "There's a small group of sitting representatives in Congress. They're calling for big change, like Michelle. They're focused on calling out corruption and working with grassroots groups to get rid of everyone in the party who isn't working for the people. They're bringing attention to the alliances they have with lobbyists, corporations, even foreign countries. They're powerful people with powerful friends. One of the loudest among them, a guy from Georgia. He was on television, shining the light on them, and the next thing you know, his daughter dies in an accident." Randy used air quotes.

"Her car drove into some sort of pond on their property, and she drowned. He resigned his seat the next day." He raised his brows at Coop. "These people don't take kindly to being threatened or exposed."

"So, are you saying one of these powerful people in Congress could be behind Michelle's murder?"

Randy shrugged. "I don't know, but it was made clear to me they didn't want her running."

"Back to my initial question. Did you encounter Michelle or visit the library?"

He shook his head. "No, I saw Michelle before dinner. We didn't talk. I guess you could say we glared at each other, but we didn't have a conversation. She could be volatile, and I didn't want to risk a scene at an event like that one."

"Did you notice anyone enter or leave the library when you were going to or from the music room?"

His eyes drifted upwards as he thought. "I don't remember seeing anyone, but I wasn't focused on that. It was a bad night for me."

"Where were you when Victoria made the announcement to return to your table due to a medical emergency?"

"Marcus and I had finished our conversation by then. I was just leaving the restroom and walking into the Great Hall and back to our table."

"And Marcus? Was he with you?"

With a shake of his head, he said, "No. I left the music room first. He stayed behind to make a call."

"I've heard you're planning to resign your position over all this?"

His shoulders slumped, and Randy hung his head. "Yeah, I've been encouraged by everyone in the party that it's for the best. I'm the one who will take the fall for all of it."

Coop waited for Randy to lift his head and met his eyes. "Randy, did you kill or arrange for the murder of Michelle?"

His mouth gaped open. "No, no, I would never do that. It's no secret, we didn't get along, and the audio release was a threat to my career, but I would never kill her." His voice got quieter. "I didn't like her and didn't want her to run. She was horrible for the party. I've probably wished her dead, like we all say in a joking way, but I never meant it."

"I understand your wife Elana is a doctor and professor of medicine?"

He frowned. "That's right."

"She wasn't at the gala, is that correct? She didn't show up late or anything and meet you outside?"

The crease in Randy's forehead deepened. "No. She was at a fundraiser for the university that night."

"Does she bring drugs, syringes, and such home with her?"

"She's got a doctor's bag that she's always carried. I know there are syringes in it, and I'm sure there are medications, but I don't know the specifics."

"Did you have occasion to access that bag or any of the medications in it?"

"I'm not sure what you're suggesting."

"Michelle was murdered by a fatal dose of succinylcholine. Your wife has access to such a drug and would know how it works. I'm trying to ascertain if you have access to it or could have gained access to it with or without her knowledge."

A scarlet streak rose from Randy's neck and colored his face. "I am beyond offended that you would even suggest such a horrible thing. I had nothing to do with Michelle's death. I have no idea if my wife has the drug in her bag. I would have no idea how to use it, even if she did. Elana would never violate her oath and provide me or anyone else with it to be used as a weapon."

His voice was shaking as he stood. "I resent this line of questioning. I want you to leave right now. I've said all I'm going to say."

Coop held up his hands. "Mr. Boone, you must understand I have to ask these questions, and the police will be asking similar ones. You had a strong motive, you were in the area of the murder, and you may, I stress, may have had access to the murder weapon via your wife. It's not a stretch to ask you about these things."

"I don't care," he spat. "I'm tired of being the fall guy for everything. I might have to lose my job over what Michelle did, but I didn't kill her, and I'm not going to be the scapegoat for murder."

He stomped toward the front door and opened it wide. "I won't be talking to you again, Mr. Harrington. You can speak to my lawyer if you need further answers."

Coop slipped a business card between his fingers and

held it out to Randy. "Have your attorney call me. What's his name?"

Randy glanced at the card and let it fall to the floor. He didn't say another word and as soon as Coop stepped over the threshold, he slammed the door.

CHAPTER FOURTEEN

F riday morning, Coop loaded Gus into the Jeep and headed to Peg's Pancakes for breakfast with Ben. Their new patio was open and dog friendly, which resulted in much tail wagging from Gus as Coop led him to their new favorite table tucked into a quiet corner. Gus sprawled across the cool concrete under the shade of a tree next to Coop's chair.

As soon as one of the young staff members delivered a big bowl of water for Gus, Ben arrived. He spotted Coop and waved as he made his way to the table. Myrtle, their favorite waitress, wasn't a fan of traipsing outside and with her seniority, opted to serve indoor guests, but she made one exception for her favorite Friday breakfast duo.

Ben gave Gus a quick scratch behind his ears and slid into the chair across from Coop. As soon as he turned his coffee cup over, Myrtle appeared with the pot of dark liquid that always brought a smile to Coop's face. "What sounds good this mornin', boys? We've got a special on the strawberry pancake stack with eggs and bacon."

"Sold," said Coop. "I'll take one to go for AB, too."

Ben nodded. "Sounds good to me."

Myrtle smiled. "You two make it easy on me. That's why you're my favorites. Be right back."

Coop stirred sugar into his mug, and Ben took his first sip of coffee and sighed. "What a week, huh?"

After a long swallow of his favorite Brew, Coop grinned. "I hear ya. It was nonstop yesterday with interviews for me. The only suspect left on our list to interview is the husband, Joe."

Ben nodded. "We've talked to him but didn't learn much. So many times, it's the husband." He shrugged. "This time, though, I don't see how he could have done it."

Coop swallowed a long sip. "From what I can see, he's got a tight alibi from everyone at the table during the murder window."

"Exactly. We haven't been able to come up with anybody. It's frustrating with so many people at a scene."

Coop glanced down at Gus, who was resting his eyes. "Daniel Prescott admitted to going into the library at Michelle's invitation, but he says she was alive and well when he left her."

Ben raised his brows. "I've read all the reports and didn't see that information in our file. We obviously didn't press him hard enough."

"I told you I heard a rumor that Daniel and Michelle were having an affair. I talked to him yesterday, and he confirmed it. Said it was over, just a workplace fling, but she was at the door of the library and waved him inside. She showed him her new campaign website and wanted his advice. I think he's embarrassed about the affair."

"What do you think? Is he believable?"

Coop nodded. "I believed him. We dug in further and if he's telling the truth, the murder window is between 8:20 and when we found Michelle at 8:27."

Ben shook his head. "Too bad there aren't cameras in the chateau."

"Then we wouldn't have the fun of this crazy puzzle." Coop winked as Myrtle appeared with her arms loaded down with their breakfast platters.

With the arrival of their food, Gus' nose rose. Myrtle slipped a saucer of scrambled eggs from the plates she carried and placed it in front of the dog. "I couldn't forget my favorite furry friend."

She glanced at their cups. "I'll grab more coffee for y'all."

Moments later, Myrtle refilled their cups, and they dug into the stack of pancakes topped with juicy berries and whipped cream.

Ben took a quick sip from his cup. "Who told you about Michelle's affair with Daniel?"

Coop grinned. "A very trusted source. Daniel tried to play dumb at first, but then he caved right away and explained it. Honestly, I don't think he's our guy. He regrets the relationship."

Ben nodded. "Randy Boone is the one who keeps popping up on my radar."

"Same," Coop said, spearing another bite of fluffy pancake. "I saw him last night, and he was beyond tense. He's pretty paranoid, but it could be for good reason. Told me powerful people in Congress didn't want Michelle to run. Told me a story about a politician in Georgia who was on television shining the light on corruption within the party, and the next thing he heard was the guy's daughter drowned in a freak accident on their ranch. He resigned his position in Congress. Then, Randy booted me out of his house when I asked about his wife and her access to succinylcholine."

Coop slipped Gus a strawberry and wiped his fingers on a napkin. "Did you find any fingerprints at the scene?"

Ben shook his head. "Nothing usable. The prints on the door were smeared, except for those of the owners and their staff. We did find one of Michelle's on the glass pane of the door. Only Michelle's on her phone and the champagne glass. Nothing to point us to anyone else."

"Her fingerprint on the glass matches with Daniel's story of her asking him inside to look at her phone."

Coop swallowed another sip from his cup. "It's one of those cases with too many viable suspects but nothing concrete to implicate one of them. *Cui bono?* That old phrase of who benefits keeps coming back to me. Her husband is the first one who comes to mind, of course. Randy's got me thinking about bigger players in the political arena, though. AB is going to do a little undercover work and plans to visit Zen to get a feel for Joe. We heard he's involved with the manager of the Green Hills location, Paula Kinkade."

Ben nodded as he finished chewing. "We heard the same. Haven't been able to confirm it yet. Joe denies it."

"I'm going to let AB snoop around a bit before we call him for an interview. I also need to update Victoria and Arthur. I was hoping to be much further along by now."

"You and me both, brother. I hate these high-profile cases with the press bugging us every minute for an update. Oddly, that's the only real pressure we're getting. Usually, the family is all over us, but in this case, they've been quiet. I think Victoria and Arthur have called more than anyone else."

Coop shrugged. "Our victim wasn't the warm and fuzzy type or particularly likeable. Estranged from her daughter and not involved in her life. Very few, what I would call, friends. Several business and political colleagues, but none of them appear overly distressed by the news. Truthfully, Daniel seemed the most upset about her death. Nobody I've talked to has been brokenhearted, apart from Bridget. From what I've learned, they weren't close, but like any kid who loses a parent, it's impactful, no matter what."

Ben's phone sounded, and he reached for it and tapped the screen. He arched his brows as he caught Coop's eye. "Kate said the press release just dropped, and Randy Boone is stepping down as chair of the party."

Coop reached for his coffee. "No way he was gonna survive that audio leak. It was just a matter of when. He seemed genuinely worried last night when he was talking about those in power." Coop shrugged. "Knowing how politics works, he'll probably get a promotion and more money or end up working as a lobbyist."

"He's a guy with plenty of motive himself," said Ben.

"I agree and a wife in the medical field who would have access to the drug."

"Good theory. If only we could prove it."

Coop smiled at Myrtle, who poured hot coffee into their cups and collected Gus' empty saucer.

After adding more sugar to his cup, Coop glanced at Ben and lowered his voice. "What about access to succinylcholine? I thought I was onto something with Adam Marshall, the ex-husband's son being a doctor, but his alibi seems solid. From what you've learned, how hard is it to obtain?"

With a shake of his head, Ben said, "It's prevalent in medical settings. I've had a team visiting clinics, hospitals, urgent care centers. They haven't found a smoking gun, so to speak, yet. I'm not sure the accounting is foolproof, so I don't know if we'll ever find where it came from. If we found a vial or something, we might be able to trace it. The killer was brazen enough to bring it and leave with it, all while staying calm enough to get it out of the chateau. No idea where it went from there."

"Yeah, definitely takes some steady nerves, especially since the police showed up to interview people."

"Doesn't help that we didn't know what we were dealing with that night." Ben wiped his mouth with his napkin and slugged down the rest of his coffee. "I better get a move on. This Randy thing will invite more speculation about the case. As you know, we've got other cases, so I can't afford to keep a huge number of detectives on this one. If you learn anything from Joe or AB's undercover work, let me know."

"Will do, Ben. I'll be in touch. I plan to go to the celebration of life next week. Hoping it's solved by then, but if not, I want to check out the people who attend."

Ben smiled and started to dig out his wallet. Coop shook his head and said, "I've got it. Your turn next week."

With a quick stop to give Gus a pet, Ben made his way to the exit.

Coop lingered as he sipped his coffee and waited for AB's breakfast, while the list of suspects cycled through his mind.

———

When Coop and Gus got to the office, AB was at her desk. She welcomed the takeout box, and Gus stationed himself at her feet, waiting for any nibble she deigned to share. Coop noticed her black yoga pants and workout wear, not to mention her dark hair and baseball cap.

She smiled at him. "I thought I'd put on a little disguise for my trip to Zen, just in case." She whipped out a pair of thick, black-rimmed glasses and added them.

"Perfect. You look totally different than you did at the gala."

Coop wandered into his office and reviewed the white board. He made a new suspect column based on the proximity to the murder. It contained Emily Harper, Marcus Ryle, Randy Boone, Daniel Prescott, and Bridget Marshall. They were all without a firm alibi for the time of the murder. Of those, he circled Randy's name. He had the most to gain, along with Marcus. He also added a question mark and noted unknown political operative next to it.

As he pondered, AB came through the door. "Brian from Daniel Prescott's office is due in a few minutes. He's the last one we need to interview, except for Joe Ward."

"Okay, I'll watch for him. You can head down to Zen and see what you can learn about Paula and Joe. After you report back, I'll give him a call and set up an interview. I want you to observe him in his natural state without the worry of an interview hanging over his head."

"Sounds good." AB pointed at her jacket that matched her pants and shirt. "I added a buttonhole camera. It'll record to my phone and upload to our cloud account automatically."

"Perfect, I'll keep an eye on it while you're there. If you run into trouble, just make an excuse and leave. Don't take any chances."

She rolled her eyes. "I think I'll be fine, but I appreciate the thought."

Coop and Gus walked her to the back door and watched her climb behind the wheel of her bright-green VW Bug. Coop glanced down at Gus and put his hand on the dog's soft head. "She'll be okay, big guy."

A few minutes later, Brian arrived. He shook Coop's hand, and Coop offered him a seat on the couch in reception.

He declined the offer of something to drink, his foot tapping on the floor as he awaited Coop's questions.

"I'm sure Mr. Prescott shared that we're talking with everyone who attended the gala and had a relationship with Ms. Roberts, looking into her murder."

Brian nodded. "Yes, he mentioned he came for an interview with you and the police, of course. The police already talked to me."

"I understand. From what I know from the others at your table, you stayed there and didn't play the murder mystery game or go anywhere once the game started. I'm looking for anything you might have noticed or observed while you were there, specifically, near the library. Did you see anyone coming or going from it or did anyone give you pause?"

He shook his head. "I just know Congressman Ryle and Mr. Boone left the table, as did Daniel. I think Mrs. Winters also left." He paused and moment and added, "Yeah, she did. I didn't leave the table, so I'm not sure about the library. I was mostly on my phone until they announced the paramedics were there and asked everyone to take their seats. I didn't notice anything that comes to mind."

"What did you think of Ms. Roberts? Did you work with her much?"

His eyes widened. "I did work with her, scheduling meetings, providing information, and such. She was, uh, demanding. Not someone you wanted to keep waiting."

"I'm sure you've heard about the audio Michelle leaked of her conversation with Randy Boone."

Brian nodded. "It was a hot topic."

"Did Randy mention it the night of the gala?"

"Oh, yeah. He and Marcus were upset about it. Randy was fuming all night. He downplayed it but slammed back drinks."

"When everyone heard that Michelle was dead, did anyone's reaction surprise you?"

He frowned. "No, not really. I didn't pay that much attention. I knew Governor Brown would need to put out some sort of statement, so I worked on that with Daniel. It was a surprise for sure. Most everyone seemed to be in shock from what I remember."

Coop chatted for a few more minutes and after learning nothing more, he thanked Brian for his time.

With an eye on the clock, Coop took a few minutes and called Victoria Sinclair. He hated telling her they hadn't solved the case yet but assured her they were working every angle. He expected the tone of disappointment he heard in her voice, but she was cordial and thanked him.

With that task done, Coop hurried to his office and logged onto his computer, anxious to check out the story about the congressman from Georgia who Randy mentioned.

After a quick search, he found the incident Randy mentioned. It happened earlier in the year. He scanned several articles that mentioned the story and dug into the politician who had resigned. He was new to Congress and like Randy said, was doing everything he could to shine the light on the leadership of his own party and those who were selling out the American people to foreign interests and lobbyists.

He was young, vocal, and maniacally focused. Every interview he gave or article he wrote, he pounded on what he called the establishment politicians who worked to line their own pockets instead of representing the American people.

Like Randy said, he resigned the day after his daughter's

death. His statement was short and stated his family needed him at this tragic time.

Coop made a note to crosscheck the guest list with anyone affiliated with Congress, including lobbyists. If it was someone sent from leadership in D.C., things would get intense.

CHAPTER FIFTEEN

Coop turned his attention to AB's camera feed. As it came up on his screen, a woman came into view. She was decked out in black and teal exercise clothing, emblazoned with the Zen logo. Someone walked by and called her Paula, which made Coop perk up and pay attention. Her dark hair was in a perky ponytail, and she had a nonstop smile to go with her trim figure. She was showcasing the locker room and pointing out the amenities.

He tuned Paula out as she explained all the private showers were down the hall. Next, she led AB down a large hallway and touted the sauna, steam room, and hydrotherapy treatment rooms. She explained the various types of massage therapies, body wraps, and facials they offered.

Coop's eyes glazed over as she named all the different body scrubs and polishers available to clients, along with waxing and aromatherapy. After asking if AB had any questions, Paula led her through a locked set of double doors, which she opened with a keycard.

"This is our Med Spa, where we do more intensive

procedures, including a variety of laser treatments and injectables such as fillers and neuromodulators. We're especially proud of our microneedling, fibro blasting, and exosome therapies. All these therapies are supervised by a medical doctor, and our excellent technicians are all highly trained."

Coop was glad AB asked what some of the treatments involved, since he had no idea. Paula explained about using specialized tools to make small wounds in the skin to stimulate cell turnover and collagen. "All these treatments are designed to tighten and enhance the skin and are used as wonderful alternatives to the traditional surgical procedures. Clients have much less downtime and risks."

Paula led AB down the long hallway where a few women dressed in black and teal scrubs passed by as they entered rooms. Paula stopped and showed AB the interior of a few of the different treatment rooms, with fancy-looking specialized chairs and beds for patients. All of them were sleek and modern with high-tech equipment Coop had never seen.

As Coop listened to Paula describe the needling procedure, he shivered. He couldn't imagine willingly undergoing any of the treatments she described. When AB asked about the cost, he nearly fell off his chair.

No wonder Zen was a money maker.

As they left the Med Spa area, they walked back to the main reception desk. Paula pointed at another set of doors. "We've got a lovely atrium area for relaxing with an outdoor space. Right now, the owner, Joe, is setting up for a memorial celebration we're having next week. His poor wife passed away last week."

AB gasped. "Oh, my. That's horrible."

"Yes, we're all struggling with the news, and Joe is so

strong and powering through his grief. He wants to honor Michelle and make sure the event is special. We're having a celebration of her life and a sort of open house." She opened the door and motioned AB through it. "We'll just take a quick look so you can see the space."

As they walked in, AB turned her torso to capture the stocky man in the corner, fiddling with wires and cables connected to the audio-visual system. Coop recognized Joe from the gala and their background reports. Paula waved her hand around the space. "We've moved out the lounge chairs and small tables and brought in all these tables and chairs for the service, but normally, clients can use the space to relax, read, even take a nap. We can open the roof on warm days. It's lovely, and the hot tub is just through that archway."

The man turned, and Paula said, "Joe, we'll be out of your way in a few minutes. I'm just showing a prospective client, Anna, around the place."

"Take your time," Joe said, with a smile.

Paula led AB outside to the patio area she mentioned, surrounded by high walls and filled with plants and trees. "Again, you'd normally find lounge chairs and such out here, but we've moved all of them to set up for the event."

AB turned toward a large fountain in the center of the space where the gentle fall of the water cascading over the rim made for a peaceful sound. Coop felt his shoulders relax as he listened and took in the serene space.

"It's lovely," said AB, turning back to Paula.

"Once the memorial service is over, things will be back to normal. Joe has been such a trooper. We're all helping him as much as possible."

"Have you worked here a long time?" AB asked.

Paula nodded. "I've been here since the start. Joe hired me to manage this location. I think I mentioned we have four other sites in the area. If you decide to join, your membership is good at any of the locations. The other locations are smaller, without the Med Spa, though."

AB took several steps toward the door to the atrium. "I will definitely give it some thought. It's very tempting."

Paula held the door for her, and they went back into the atrium. Photos of Michelle flashed onto the large flatscreen on the wall. AB turned toward Paula, and Coop noticed her perpetual smile was gone. AB pointed at the screen. "She was a beautiful woman and looked so young. What a shame."

Paula nodded but continued to stare at the screen. "Yes, she was very attractive for her age."

Joe wandered toward them, checking the view and sound from the furthest corners of the room. As he stood near them, AB cleared her throat. "I'm very sorry for you loss."

He turned and nodded at AB. "Thank you. Michelle was bigger than life. I'm not sure how we'll manage without her." The words rang true, but his facial expression didn't change. He looked neither happy nor sad, just intent on his project.

Paula inched closer to him and put a hand on his shoulder. "Joe has been so strong during all of this. He's quite the marvel." She smiled up at him with adoration.

Coop's brows rose as he witnessed their interaction. Joe was a handsome enough guy, in that gym rat, muscular way many women seemed to like. Clearly, Paula was a fan.

Joe smiled at her. "Just keeping busy. We'll get through this, I'm sure." He reached out and squeezed the top of Paula's shoulder.

Paula gazed at Joe for a few moments and then pointed back toward the main reception area. "Well, I've got some brochures for you at the desk and a discount coupon for a spa treatment, so you can try us out, with a day pass you can use for the gym. Hopefully, we've impressed you enough to join us."

AB followed her through the double doors, where she collected a folder filled with brochures and her discount and complimentary pass. "Thanks so much for the tour, Paula. I'll be sure to come back and try it out before I make a decision."

"Wonderful to meet you, Anna. You take care now. Hope to see you soon."

AB turned toward the exit and walked across the parking lot and through the adjoining property to her car, where she whispered, "On my way back, Coop. See you in a few."

As soon as she got in her car, the feed disconnected, and Coop stared at Gus. "What do you make of Paula and Joe? They seemed a little more than co-workers to me."

Gus thumped his tail across the leather chair.

———

By the time AB returned, Coop had leftover ham sandwiches, courtesy of Aunt Camille, on the kitchen table, along with some homemade potato salad and cookies. The first thing AB did was remove the dark wig she was wearing.

Gus stood in awe, his head cocked, as he watched her.

"It's okay, big guy," said Coop, reaching out to pet him. "It's still our AB under there."

She laughed and put the wig back into the bag and ran her fingers over her scalp. "I don't know how people wear wigs fulltime. They're annoying."

"Well, you looked great. Totally unrecognizable." He retrieved the pitcher of sweet tea from the fridge and poured each of them a glass. "I tuned in as she was showing you the locker room."

AB nodded and dug into her sandwich. "You just missed the actual gym and group class area. Nothing much."

"It looks like a pretty high-end operation, especially all the stuff in the Med Spa."

She nodded and slipped the folder across the table. "I would say they're making a pretty penny. Check out the fees for those treatments and the membership plans. Out of my price range for sure."

With his eyes wide as he took in the fee schedule, Coop nibbled on his sandwich and washed it down with a long swallow of tea. "What was your take on Joe and Paula?"

AB's brows rose. "I definitely get a friends-with-benefits vibe from them. She seems almost infatuated with him. Neither of them seems distraught about Michelle's death. It seems like more of an excuse to showcase the business. I mean who has an open house with a celebration of life?"

Coop's brow furrowed. "Yeah, I picked up on that, too."

AB cocked her head. "I know Joe has an alibi for the time of the murder. He couldn't have done it, but there is something hinky about him. And Paula. It's just weird."

As Coop wiped his hands on a napkin, he nodded. "Yeah, something doesn't sit right. When Paula mentioned they have a doctor overseeing their treatments and the injectables and all that, it makes me think we need to take a closer look at the staff at Zen. Just a double check to see if any of them have a relationship with anyone at the gala."

She blew out a breath. "That's a huge undertaking."

"Yeah, I know, and it could be a total waste of time. I also checked out that story about the congressman in Georgia Randy told me about. We need to crosscheck the guest list against anyone affiliated with lobbyists or Congress in D.C. Let's call Madison and Ross in and have them do surveillance on Joe and Paula. They can help with the research on the staff at Zen, too. I'm curious about how Joe is spending his time now that Michelle is dead. I'm going to call Joe and set up an interview."

AB slipped Gus a tiny bite of ham and carried their plates to the sink. "I'll call Madison and Ross and get them on it. With Victoria willing to cover whatever costs are necessary, it makes sense. I can check out the guest list and flag anyone with a D.C. connection."

Coop finished the last scoop of potato salad before he washed the bowl and left it on the counter to take back to Aunt Camille.

Once back at his desk, he called Joe's cell phone, and, after passing on his condolences, Coop asked to meet with him at his earliest convenience. Joe's tone was less than enthusiastic as he reminded Coop he'd already spoken with the police, and he was busy setting up the memorial service at Zen. Coop offered to meet him there, promising it wouldn't take long.

Joe finally relented and said he could meet him on Sunday morning.

With that settled, Coop studied the white board. The four most likely suspects were circled in red—Marcus, Randy, Daniel, and Emily. They had the most to gain from Michelle's death. The unknown political operative was also a possibility, but there was no way to eliminate any of them since they were all in the area during the time of the murder. As much as Coop despised Marcus, he didn't think he did it, and Emily didn't seem like a likely candidate. He also believed Daniel and didn't see a strong motive there. Randy was the most likely, and everyone agreed he was furious with Michelle. But did his anger and fury prompt him to inject her with a lethal dose of a drug? His wife would have access, but would she facilitate it?

He consulted the background report on Randy and put in a call to Elana Boone. Her voicemail asked him to leave a message, and he did so, asking her to call as soon as possible. Certain that Randy had already warned her off, Coop didn't hold out much hope for a prompt return call. He added her office address in his notepad and envisioned an in-person visit would be necessary.

After studying the suspect list again, he turned his attention to the herculean task of checking the details of the staff members at Zen. With Anthony Carlisle's help, he obtained a list of employees, including the dermatologist who oversaw all the medical procedures at Zen. He and AB spent the afternoon combing through them for any connection to the guests or catering staff in attendance at the gala.

Within a couple of hours, Madison and Ross arrived, and they reported they had already installed trackers on both Joe and Paula's vehicles. They were both still at Zen in Green Hills, but they were prepared to follow each of them when they left, and their phones would alert them to any movement.

With Coop's eyes tired from sifting through the online reports for the staff at Zen, he reached for his cell phone to call Ben.

"Hey, Coop," he answered.

"Sorry to bug you. AB did some snooping at Zen today, and we think it's worth learning more about Paula and Joe. They seem a little too friendly with each other. When she visited and saw all the procedures they offer with injections and needling, which sounds like torture to me, it made us think. We're going through the staff there now to make sure there are no connections to someone at the gala. I'm just curious if you looked into the Med Spa doctor at Zen. Dr.

Ariel St. Clair is her name. From what I know, dermatologists don't use succinylcholine but wasn't sure."

"Good idea. Let me check with Kate. She's been running point on this one. I'll call you back."

A few minutes before five, AB rushed through his door. "Madison got a ping on Paula's vehicle. She's going to follow it and let us know what she learns. Ross is heading out to get in position to follow Joe if he moves."

AB volunteered to stay late, and they had a pizza delivered as they studied the backgrounds on the two dozen employees at Zen and looked for connections to lobbyists or operatives in D.C. In the midst of their work, Madison texted to let them know Paula, with her purse dog, had visited a restaurant, collected takeout, and was now at Joe's house, where he had gone after leaving Zen.

As AB read the text, her brows arched. "I'm sure they're just working hard on Michelle's memorial, right?" She tapped her phone and added, "It gets better. Paula brought her dog and parked her car in the garage. Joe left his outside in the driveway."

Coop reached for another piece of pizza and chuckled. "Sounds like they're planning an all-nighter."

"Madison and Ross are going to split the overnight shift, and they'll keep us updated. They think they're in for the evening."

After reading the background on Dr. St. Clair again, Coop shook his head. "I don't see anything that gives me pause on her. She worked in a dermatology practice prior to going to Zen, but she's got a clean record, nothing obvious to connect her to anyone on the guest list. She'd probably have connections to other doctors, plastic surgeons and such, who would have access to the drug, but that's a tenuous connection, at best."

Coop's phone rang with a call from Ben. After a short conversation, he disconnected. "Kate's team researched if succinylcholine is used in dermatology, and it's not. It's limited to surgical procedures and patients who need intubation. Like we thought."

With a yawn, AB nodded. "I can come in tomorrow and keep going on this, but I need to call it a night. I can't see straight."

"Sounds good. I'll see you in the morning, and we should be able to finish it up. I'll see if Victoria can help us narrow down the list with connections to anyone in D.C. She'd know that more than anyone."

Coop made the short trip back to Camille's, where Gus made a mad dash for the couch he favored in the family sitting room. Coop found a note from Camille, letting him know she and Charlie went to a movie.

Coop slipped onto the couch next to Gus, who was sprawled atop the buttery soft blanket Camille bought for him, and rubbed his head. He leaned against the back of the couch and shut his eyes, letting the facts he'd garnered percolate.

He replayed his conversations with the suspects. Was someone lying or was he missing something? Or both?

As he drifted to sleep, his cell phone rang out and startled him. He squinted at the screen, surprised to see Darcy Flint's name. His stomach knotted as his finger hovered over the green button. The lawyer from Vermont calling at this hour didn't bode well.

"Ms. Flint," he answered.

"Mr. Harrington, I'm sorry to call so late. It's about your mother. I just got a call from the jail. They've taken your mother to the hospital. I thought you'd want to know."

CHAPTER SIXTEEN

S he gave him the name of the hospital and the number to the jail. "If I can help in any way, please let me know."

He thanked her and disconnected. With a long sigh, he contemplated his next step. As much as Marlene drove him nuts, he didn't wish any harm to come to her. He stared at his phone for several minutes and then tapped in the number to the hospital in Vermont.

He finally got transferred to the emergency room nurse's station. The nurse explained his mother had been transported by ambulance after complaining of symptoms of a heart attack. The doctors were assessing his mother and as soon as she knew anything definitive, she would call him back.

Coop thanked her and disconnected. He scrolled online for flight information. No direct flights, of course. Tomorrow, there were a handful of seats left on a morning flight and one on the afternoon flight. The last thing he needed right now was an impromptu trip that would take the better part of a day. Not to mention, spending time with Marlene.

He shut his eyes, waiting to hear how serious her situation was before he made a reservation.

Marlene's timing never failed. She always managed to pop up when Coop was the busiest. He couldn't miss the interview with Joe on Sunday. If he made the trip to Vermont tomorrow, there was no way he would make it home in time.

He trusted AB with his life, and she could handle the interview, but the disguise she used when she visited Zen wouldn't hold up to a long conversation with him. The only option might be a flight on Sunday afternoon, but then he'd miss the celebration of life, where he hoped to learn more by observing those in attendance.

As he wandered into the kitchen and paced the floor before giving in and making a pot of coffee, his phone chimed. Ross, who was on the overnight shift, provided a quick update. Paula was still at Joe's, and the lights had just gone off in the house. He suspected no more activity but would stay put until Madison relieved him in the morning.

Coop replied with a quick emoji and poured himself a large cup of the freshly brewed coffee he craved. There was no way he would sleep tonight anyway.

It didn't say much about his relationship with his mother that he was prioritizing a case over her health, but that was his reality. Marlene had stopped being his mom long ago. He would drop anything to help his dad, but his mom was less than a stranger to him.

He sipped from his mug while he stared at the clock.

Gus gave up and curled onto his bed. He had no trouble sleeping through Coop's nighttime antics. Coop joined Gus in the sitting room where Aunt Camille and Charlie spent most of their evenings watching television. As he scrolled through viewing options, Gus' ears perked, and he hurried from the room.

By the time Gus led Charlie and Camille to the sitting room, Coop was on the phone with the hospital.

"Thanks, Doctor. I understand and appreciate you calling me." Coop disconnected and slipped the phone back in his pocket.

Charle and Camille stood staring at him. Charlie spoke first, "What's that about, son? Everything okay?"

"I got a call a couple of hours ago that they transported Marlene to the hospital with symptoms of a heart attack."

"Oh, no," said Camille, taking a seat in her usual chair.

"That was the ER doctor. He said they ran a bunch of tests to make sure, but it was a panic attack. They're going to send her back to jail tonight."

Charlie sighed. "Well, that's good news."

Coop shrugged. "Yeah, I was sitting here dreading the idea of flying up there to see her and taking time away from this case. She's hard to care about, but I still feel like a heel for thinking that."

Charlie took a seat on the same couch as Coop. "It's understandable. Marlene doesn't make it easy. It's no fun being the one who has to pick up the pieces after she storms through."

Coop yawned. "I'm beat. It's been a long week, and I'm working this weekend, trying to get a handle on this case." He rose from the couch, taking his empty cup with him. "Good night. See you two in the morning."

"Sleep well, Coop," said Aunt Camille.

Like the loyal friend he was, Gus followed Coop to his wing of the house. By the time Coop crawled into bed, Gus was fast asleep, sprawled across the chair in the corner.

As Coop tossed and turned, thoughts about the murder case mingled with memories of his mother. He longed to quiet his racing mind and for the sweet solace of sleep. It was always elusive, but stress took it to another level.

———

Saturday morning, Coop's eyes struggled to open. He squinted to look at the clock. It was after nine o'clock. The last time he remembered checking the time, it was three in the morning.

He peered over at Gus' chair, but it was empty. No doubt, Gus was enjoying breakfast in the company of his dad and Aunt Camille. He picked up his cell phone from the nightstand and saw two messages from Madison. The first one was when she checked in at six in the morning, letting Coop know there had been no activity all night, and Ross was going home to catch a few hours of sleep.

The second message was about thirty minutes ago, reporting that both Joe and Paula left the house in separate vehicles, and Madison followed them to Zen in Green Hills. She was stationed in a nearby parking lot, waiting for any further activity.

Coop stumbled into the shower and let the warm water loosen his muscles and rain over his head.

By the time he emerged and found his way to the kitchen, Coop felt better and up to facing what would be a long day of work. As he rounded the corner, he heard AB's laugh. She and Charlie were seated at the island counter.

"Morning," said Coop, reaching for a mug from the cupboard. Aunt Camille was closest to the coffeemaker and smiled as she poured him a fresh brew.

She returned the carafe. "I was just going to wake you. I've got breakfast in the oven, and it's almost done."

Coop sniffed the air, detecting a hint of chocolate. "Did you make your double chocolate chunk muffins?"

Aunt Camille beamed. "Yes, I did. After last night, I thought you needed a little treat. We've got that ham and cheese breakfast casserole you and Charlie love and muffins. I called AB and told her since y'all had to work this weekend, she should come and join us for a hearty breakfast."

AB chuckled. "She didn't have to twist my arm very hard. She had me at chocolate muffins."

The oven timer dinged, and Coop grabbed the potholders and took out the casserole and muffin pan for Aunt Camille. She pointed at the stack of plates and utensils on the island counter. "Nothing fancy this mornin'. It's a serve yourself kind of breakfast."

Coop dished up the cheesy casserole onto plates, while Camille popped the muffins onto a serving plate and set them on the counter. The four of them dug into the delicious meal and chatted about their plans for the weekend.

Coop and AB had nothing planned beyond work at the office, which they hoped to finish before dinner. Camille and Charlie were signed up to play in a game tournament at the Community Center. Along with bingo, mahjong, poker, and canasta, lunch was included, so they would be busy all day.

After breakfast, Coop volunteered to do the dishes and tidy the kitchen so Charlie and Camille could get to the center early. AB pitched in and helped him load the dishwasher.

As she added the leftover muffins to a container, AB said, "Did you see the update from Madison? Sounds like Joe detoured to a coffee place and arrived later than Paula. They're still trying to pretend they aren't together."

Coop nodded. "Yeah, I saw that. They're both brazen and cowardly at the same time."

"If everyone hadn't confirmed Joe never left the table, I would bet you a hundred bucks he did it." AB wrinkled her nose. "Even if he didn't do it, he's a disgusting jerk. His wife's been dead a week, and he's having his girlfriend over to stay the night. Little perky Paula is a tramp, too."

"I agree they're both jerks, not to mention complete boneheads for flaunting their affair so soon after Michelle's death. No doubt, she wouldn't take home the wife of the year award either. It seems both were unfaithful."

"I know everyone acts like an age gap doesn't matter, but I've seen far too many marriages dissolve, especially when the man is so much younger than the woman. I guess men must have their heads turned more easily by youth and beauty."

Coop finished wiping the counter and chuckled. "Let's not paint all men with the same brush, AB. I would argue that those marriages were probably not based on anything substantial or a true and deep love for one another. Then, again, I watched my parents' marriage implode. I chalk that up to my mom being batshit crazy."

"Your dad is a total sweetheart and yes, your mom is off the charts." She and Gus followed Coop to his wing of the house.

When he opened the door to his bedroom, she frowned. "When is the last time you tidied up in here?"

He sighed. "Mrs. Henderson tried to get in here last week, but I told her to leave it. As you know, we've been a little busy this past week, so my good intentions went by the wayside."

AB stood, her hands on her hips. "Get a clean set of

sheets, and I'll help you change the bed." She poked her head into his bathroom. "And some fresh towels while you're at it."

By the time he returned with the sheets and stripped the bed, AB had the bathroom sparkling and hung the clean towels on the racks.

As AB furled the sheet across the bed, she pointed at the corner. "Be sure to get that all the way under the mattress."

He saluted her. "Yes, ma'am. I think you missed your calling as a drill sergeant."

She laughed. "Getting back to my theory about younger men, I'll give you the point on your argument." She slipped the pillowcase over a pillow. "I didn't mean to disparage all men. I just think women would be wise to give it some thought before marrying a much younger man. I bet there are stats somewhere that show those marriages fail more than those where the couple is closer in age."

"You're probably right. Trust me, I'm no expert when it comes to relationships and, having never been married, I can't begin to comment on how much work it must be to stay together, but I think more than age, it's the foundation of the relationship. I would venture to guess Joe and Michelle didn't have a strong marriage to start with. They both seem superficial and the way she abandoned her daughter...well, it probably hits a little too close to home for me."

She redid the hospital corner on Coop's side, then they added the comforter and pillows. Coop carried the pile of laundry out the door while AB collected the empty mugs and glasses strewn around the office part of Coop's suite.

Gus, cuddled into his favorite chair, watched the progress.

AB stepped closer to him and patted his head. "At least it

doesn't look like a fourteen-year-old boy lives here now, right?"

Gus thwacked his tail against the chair while he reached out with his tongue and ran it over AB's hand.

She sniffed in the air and looked at Gus. "It still smells a little funky." She reached for the blanket draped across the dog's chair and bent to smell it. "Uh, yeah, this needs washing, too, my friend."

Coop came through the door, and AB handed him the blanket. "Gus needs a clean throw blanket, too."

He sighed and surveyed the suite. "Thanks, AB."

"At least Mrs. Henderson won't need a hazmat suit to enter." She giggled and followed Coop out the door, with Gus at her heels. "I'll meet you at the office!" she hollered, as she opened the front door.

"Be right behind you," said Coop, leading Gus to the Jeep.

It was a gorgeous spring day, and Coop glanced over at Gus. "I promise, we won't work all day and this afternoon, we'll go to the park."

Gus' ears lifted, and he gave Coop a low bark.

AB brought in her stack of research, and Coop settled in across from her at the conference table in his office. As soon as he opened the folder, the office phone rang. He turned in his chair and tried to reach the phone on the corner of his desk but had to abandon the chair.

He answered and as soon as the robotic voice asked him to accept the charges from an inmate, his shoulders slumped. He took a long breath. Whatever Marlene wanted, it beat a flight to Vermont. He agreed to pay the charges and her shrill voice came through the handset.

"Cooper, I've been calling all morning. Did you know I was at the hospital last night?"

"Yes, Ms. Flint called to let me know, and I talked to your

doctor last night. He said everything checked out, and you just had a panic attack."

"Well, of course I had a panic attack. I'm in a blasted cell. I can't stand it. I'm still not sure I didn't have a heart attack. I think the hospital is in cahoots with the cops. They just wanted me back in jail, I'm sure. It's horrible. You need to get me out of here."

Coop wished he'd opted to work from home today. "You went to court this week, right?"

"If you mean that backwards judge who doesn't give a damn about an old woman being in jail."

"As I explained to you before, and I know Ms. Flint explained to you, when you opted to violate the terms of your release from your last sentence, you'll be incarcerated to fulfill the prior sentence."

"That's all legal mumbo jumbo. I told him I'd go back to the senior center and do my community service, but he didn't want to hear it. He threatened to add more time to my sentence and told me I had a poor attitude."

Shocking. "That's because you burned your bridge. He gave you a chance, and you didn't fulfill your end of the bargain. There are no more options. You'll be in jail until your sentence is up."

"I also don't have any cigarettes. It's no wonder I had a heart attack. I'm too nervous without them."

Coop closed his eyes and willed his heart to quit racing.

"The food here is also horrible. It's like eating slop."

He continued to listen to her complain about the lack of amenities and then when she finally took a breath, he cleared his throat. "I'll put some money on your account so you can buy your cigarettes and a few things. There's nothing anyone can do at this point. You're just going to have to figure out how to pass the time for the next several weeks."

"Oh, this is awful," she wailed. Through sobs, she continued to complain about how cold she was and how much her back hurt from the thin mattress she was sure was full of bedbugs.

"I've got to go, Marlene. I'm busy here at work, but I'll call to put some money on your account right now."

"Well, a lot of good it does to have a lawyer for a son. You can't even get your poor mother out of jail. You are worthless, Coop. Totally worthless."

He couldn't respond before a loud beeping filled his ear.

He let out a breath and hung up the phone on his desk.

As he turned, AB met his eyes. "Marlene?"

"How could you tell? I'm sure you could hear her screaming voice all the way over there."

"Sorry, Coop. She's oblivious and so self-absorbed."

"I've been expecting her to call. She just makes me want to strangle her."

AB nodded. "Whatever that jailer is making up there in Vermont, it's not enough."

"Even if you added a couple more zeros to his hourly rate, it wouldn't be enough." He moved to his computer. "I better call to put some money on her account, or she'll call back."

"Safe to say, I'm not accepting any more collect calls from her?"

"Yes, for sure. If the actual jail or Ms. Flint calls, I'll speak to them, but I'm done talking to Marlene for the foreseeable future." He put in a call to the jail and got the particulars he needed to add some money to Marlene's commissary account.

With that done, he turned his attention back to the task at hand. Solving a murder was much more appealing than a conversation with his mother.

CHAPTER SEVENTEEN

By mid-afternoon, Coop called it quits. Victoria mentioned a lobbyist in attendance, a woman who had ties to a firm in D.C. Her name was Helene Brooks.

While AB ran a background on Helene Brooks, Coop scoured the backgrounds on the employees at Zen and cross referenced them against the guest list and the catering staff list. He didn't find any connections.

AB came through the door with a file on the lobbyist.

Coop opened the folder and raised his brows at AB. "What do you think?"

She shook her head. "She's got no medical connections that I can see. Her clients in Nashville are all affiliated with the music industry. I don't see any red flags, but I think it makes sense to talk to her and scratch her off the list."

Coop nodded. "I'll take the file home to study it and give her a call."

AB pointed at her phone. "Madison texted a few times to report no movement from Joe or Paula. They had been at Zen all day."

AB rinsed their cups at the sink, and Coop doused the lights. "I've had enough of beating my head on a rock for one day. Thanks for working Saturday, AB. Hopefully, you can salvage the rest of it and enjoy it."

She grinned. "Oh, yes, I have a fun-filled afternoon of laundry and grocery shopping planned."

"I promised Gus a trip to the park. If I learn anything from Joe, I'll call you tomorrow. Otherwise, I'll see you Monday."

"Remember to dress nicely. That's the celebration of life, and you'll want to blend in."

"I'll be sure to bring a change of clothes. I'm not wearing a suit all day."

AB waved as she steered her VW Bug out of the parking lot, and Coop locked the back door. Gus was already waiting at the Jeep, eager for their outing.

Coop made the short drive to Percy Warner Park and as soon as he opened the passenger door, Gus bailed out and rushed to the long stretch of grass they frequented. Coop slipped a ball from the pocket of his hoodie and threw it. Gus bounded after it and rushed back to drop it at Coop's feet.

As he threw and Gus retrieved, Coop thought of the murder case. He hadn't heard back from Elana Boone yet, so he would have to tackle her on Monday. With the way Randy acted, he preferred to chat with his wife at her workplace away from Randy. She and Joe were the last two people he needed to question.

Randy was still at the top of Coop's list of likely suspects. Michelle had humiliated him, and his livelihood was in jeopardy. The only thing that didn't make sense was the fact it wasn't a crime of passion. It wasn't someone who was enraged, grabbed the nearest weapon, and used it to kill Michelle. This was a premeditated murder.

Could Randy have heard about the leaked audio Friday night, obtained the drug, hatched a plan, and carried it out in less than twenty-four hours? Not to mention, he had to know he'd be a suspect.

As much as he detested politicians and their ilk, Coop couldn't help but think Joe had a better motive. With Michelle out of the picture, he would gain financially and personally. He had more time to plan the murder, which much to Coop's chagrin, was a near perfect crime. Randy came off more cunning and smarter, but maybe there was more to Joe than meets the eye.

After Coop's arm tired from throwing, he and Gus set out on a walk along the pathway through the trees. After a two-mile walk, Coop felt better and loaded Gus into the Jeep. When they walked through the door, the aroma of roasted chicken greeted him. Mrs. Henderson had prepped dinner and left it in the oven with a note stuck to the glass.

Coop peeked inside, and his stomach growled at the sight of the plump chicken and veggies, almost ready. He poured himself a sweet tea and detoured to his suite. As he suspected, Mrs. Henderson found his note that his room was ready for her and worked her magic. The wood floor gleamed, and the area rugs were freshly vacuumed. All traces of dust were removed, and everything was neat and orderly, with a fresh hint of citrus in the air. A stack of clean laundry, including Gus' favorite throw blanket, rested on his bed.

He wandered back out to the sitting room, where he settled into the recliner to veg out in front of the television while he waited for Charlie and Aunt Camille. There wasn't much to watch, but he couldn't resist stopping on a channel airing an older movie about a man who schemes with his mistress to kill his wife. They decide to hire a hitman, so the crime can't be linked to them.

The premise prompted Coop to think about Joe. Could he have hired someone at the gala to kill Michelle?

As he considered that angle, his phone chimed with a text from Madison. Joe and Paula were on the move again and after stopping for takeout at a different restaurant, Paula and her dog were back at Joe's with her car tucked away in the garage. Ross was due to take the night shift and would report any happenings.

———

As he was dozing off with Helene Brooks' file spread next to him, Gus jumped from Coop's lap to greet Aunt Camille and Charlie. Coop lumbered after him and found them in the kitchen, where dinner was ready and Camille had Charlie setting the table.

"How was your game tournament?" asked Coop.

Camille giggled. "I won a gift certificate to that bakery we love, and Charlie won breakfast for four at the Wet Hen."

"Wow, you guys did well. That's awesome."

Charlie smiled as he carried the pitcher of sweet tea to the table. "You find a day when it works for you and AB to join us, and we'll spend my prize."

They settled in around the table and filled their plates. "How did work go for you today, Coop?" asked Charlie.

"Marlene called me from jail, so that started the day with a bang."

Camille shook her head as she added carrots to her plate. "How is she feeling?"

"Judging from her fiery complaints and demands, I'd say just fine. She's in dire need of cigarettes and shampoo. I put some money on her commissary account."

Camille sighed. "That woman doesn't deserve you, Coop."

"Sending money is simple compared to having to talk to her or see her. Believe me, I got off easy. I told AB we won't accept any more calls from her. I'm tired of getting yelled at because I can't solve her legal problems. She's insufferable."

Charlie set his fork down and glanced over at Coop. "A stint in jail might be what she needs. She's plenty old enough to know right from wrong but has an aversion to accepting any kind of personal responsibility for her actions."

Coop raised his glass. "I'll drink to that. I think the judge feels the same way."

As they were dishing up Mrs. Henderson's banana pudding for dessert, Coop's phone rang. He frowned and excused himself from the table.

"Cooper Harrington," he answered, seeing the call was a transfer from his office phone.

"Oh, Mr. Harrington, I'm so glad you're there. This is Elana Boone. You left me a message. I'm sorry it's taken me so long to get back to you."

"Thanks so much for calling. I wanted to meet with you and ask you a few questions related to the murder of Michelle Roberts."

She sighed. "Yes, Randy told me about your visit to the house. He's livid. I'm actually at my office now and heading home soon. I was hoping you might be available to meet now. I'd rather meet you away from the house. There's a coffee shop near Vanderbilt."

Coop nodded as she mentioned a local place he knew on 21st Avenue. "Sure, I can meet you there. I'm only a few minutes away."

He apologized to his dad and Camille, who promised to wait to have their dessert with him when he returned.

The sun was setting on a gorgeous day as he pulled into the parking lot of the coffee shop. Thanks to AB's background files, he didn't have to wonder what Elana looked like and spotted her at a corner table.

The dark-haired woman, with vibrant blue eyes, smiled at him. "Mr. Harrington?"

"Yes, nice to meet you." Coop said, extending his hand as he moved the chair across from her.

Elana lowered her voice. "I appreciate you meeting me here." She shook her head and placed her hands around her cup of coffee. "I've been trying to convince Randy that I need to talk to you, but he's not in a good place and basically forbid me to meet with you."

"I'm sorry it's so stressful for you. I only have a few questions, with the first being about the drug used to kill Michelle."

"Randy told me you asked about succinylcholine. While it's true I'm familiar with it, have used it over my career, and understand how it works, I didn't obtain that drug or any other for my husband or any of his associates. I understand why he's a suspect and the logic in delving into my access and possible assistance."

Her candor shocked Coop. "You're so calm about all of it."

She shrugged. "I'm not an emotional person. I think that's part of why I excelled as a surgeon. I'm a problem solver and pretty cool under pressure. Randy, as you know, is more passionate, and this whole thing has been quite difficult for him."

"With your knowledge of it, how easy would it be to obtain it and use it as a murder weapon?"

"Even in my position at the medical school, it's not like I can just walk in and grab drugs from the hospital. There's an involved process and inventory system. I suspect it would be easier in a smaller clinic, care center, or even ambulance setting. Intubation is something that has to happen quickly and in an emergency setting, it's probably more likely that a drug or partial vial could go missing. In a surgical setting, I doubt it."

Coop pulled out his notebook. "Just for clarification, I know the audio of Randy was leaked on Friday night, to some smaller outlets. When did Randy learn about it?"

"He got some calls that night, I'd say close to eight o'clock. He was up all night, worried about the fallout. It's no secret— he didn't care for Michelle, and her latest stunt with the audio enraged him. He told me he wasn't sure he could survive it if the mainstream media picked it up."

"Saturday, the day of the gala, what did each of you do? I know you weren't with him at the gala, so where were you?"

"That morning, I tried to help by listening and even told him it might be wise to step down before it got uglier. Michelle had her mind set on taking Randy out, and I didn't see how he could whitewash the audio. I thought he should resign, save face, and look for another job. He's well connected and while I like living here, I could teach elsewhere, and we could move."

"I take it that idea didn't go over well?"

She shook her head. "No, not at all. He thought he could salvage things and going to the gala was a step on that path. He wanted to get a read on how Marcus felt and some of the donors. I was already committed to an event at the university and was there all evening. I was home before Randy, of course, with how late things ran after the incident at the gala."

"Do you think Randy took matters into his own hands with regard to Michelle and killed her?"

She shook her head. "He was furious, as I said, but I'm certain he didn't kill her. I'm almost positive he's never heard of succinylcholine until it came up in Michelle's murder.

Now, if she'd been run over in the driveway at the gala, I could maybe buy him snapping and doing something stupid. He was very threatened by her action, but I don't see how he could have come up with an elaborate plan like what it seems, overnight."

"Which is why you've come into the frame, Mrs. Boone. Someone like Randy would need help to both obtain succinylcholine and administer it."

She nodded. "I have a stellar reputation as a surgeon and professor. I would never purposely harm anyone or help someone, even my husband, kill another person. Randy has a hard time seeing past this, but he has other options. He'll eventually come to that conclusion and find another position. I give you my word and stake my reputation on it. I wasn't involved and to the best of my knowledge, neither was Randy. You can check my alibi for Saturday with the attendees at the event. I was in my office most of the day and the fundraising event in the evening. I didn't go to the hospital and have no access to that drug in my classroom setting. I'm willing to take a polygraph, if necessary."

Coop wrote down the contacts Elana had at the security office and her assistant's information, who could help with the guest list from the event, and slipped his notebook into his pocket. "Understood. I appreciate you talking with me and explaining things in such detail. One other thing Randy mentioned was the threat of those in power in Washington, D.C. He told me about the death of a Georgia representative's daughter and implied she was killed to quiet his voice that was calling out powerful people in the party. Does that ring true to you?"

She shrugged. "I remember when that happened. I don't think Randy ever had a suspect in mind, but he was convinced those in power orchestrated it. Mr. Harrington, I do my best to support my husband, but I stay far away from the details of politics. That old saying of not knowing how the sausage is made works for me. Do I think it's possible? Yes, I think absolute power corrupts, and there are those in power who will do anything to keep it. I can't help you with details, but I wouldn't be naïve enough to discount it as a conspiracy theory."

Coop nodded and reached in his pocket. "If you do think of anything that might help us narrow down how someone could obtain succinylcholine, please give me a call." He handed her his business card.

"I will. I hope you find whoever did this. I know Michelle was a thorn in my husband's side, but nobody deserves a death like she got."

Coop left her to finish her coffee and drove back to the house.

As he maneuvered through the streets of the neighborhood he knew like the back of his hand, he considered his chat with Elana. She came off as believable and trustworthy. The exact opposite of her husband. Was she the real deal or a master manipulator?

CHAPTER EIGHTEEN

Sunday, Coop woke to a clean suite and felt better than he had the last few days. AB, as usual, was right when she preached about having his environment neat and clean to alleviate unnecessary stress.

He checked his phone for text updates from Ross overnight and saw nothing to report, except a video of the two lovebirds in each other's arms outside the house. Madison had also texted to let Coop know she was in position to cover the day shift.

Coop doubted the expense of keeping them on surveillance when they weren't learning anything beyond the fact that the two of them were indeed involved and hiding it, but not doing a great job.

Coop stretched and climbed from bed. Not having the weight of travel to Vermont to tend to Marlene was a relief, as was the idea that she'd be incommunicado for the foreseeable future. After a shower, he made his bed and joined Aunt Camille and his dad in the kitchen, where Gus was already stationed.

"Good morning, Coop," said Charlie, pouring him a mug of coffee while he freshened his own cup.

"Hey, Dad. Thanks." Coop went about doctoring the mug with some sugar.

Aunt Camille waved toward the counter. "We're doing leftover muffins and casserole for breakfast. I'm prepping for supper."

"Sounds good," said Coop, helping himself to a slab of the casserole. While he waited for it to reheat in the microwave, he ate a muffin. "I've got an interview this morning at Zen in Green Hills."

"Oh, that's with the husband of the victim, right?" asked his dad.

Coop nodded as he took his plate from the microwave. "Yeah, and I hope I learn something new. This case is beginning to feel like a dead end."

Camille bustled at the counter, seasoning the pork she was planning to roast for dinner. "If I had a dollar for every time you said a case was at a dead end and turned around and solved it, I'd have a bucket of dollars. I'm sure you'll get to the bottom of it. You've been working so hard, it's no wonder you're feeling overwhelmed."

Charlie finished off the last of his muffin. "Yeah, Coop. Maybe you need a little break. I remember you saying sometimes when you let your mind wander, it comes up with the answer."

"You're right. I'll commit to taking the afternoon off and enjoying this awesome weather. Tomorrow, I've got to go to the celebration of life. Chances are the killer could be in attendance. You never know."

Camille left the roast to rest and moved onto the mixing bowls for her lemon blackberry cake. "Uncle John always went to the funeral services of his victims and if I remember correctly, he closed more than one case by doing so. Especially when the killer was someone the victim knew."

"Hopefully, Uncle John will give me some inspiration for this one. I'm beginning to think this was the perfect murder."

Coop took his empty plate and his dad's to the sink and rinsed them off before adding them to the dishwasher. He glanced over at Gus, who had his head in Charlie's lap, enjoying the ear scratches he was getting.

He sighed and said, "I don't expect I'll be too long at this interview. Maybe when I get home, we can head up to Silverwood and walk through the gardens. Didn't you say they had a jazz performance today, Aunt Camille?"

"Yes, they do. That would be wonderful, and we can take Gus as long as he's on a leash. That sounds like a perfect afternoon, Coop. We can have a bite of lunch there at the café."

"It's a date," said Coop, reaching to pet Gus. "You be a good boy and when I get back, we'll have an adventure."

Gus' tail wagged and smacked against Coop's jeans.

He didn't bother changing his shirt, lettered with I'M NOT ALWAYS RIGHT BUT I'M NEVER WRONG. Joe wasn't high on his list of people he cared about impressing.

With a promise to see them soon, Coop set out for Zen. The parking lot was almost empty, save for Joe's oversized truck that looked like he needed a step ladder to climb into it. The giant black truck was emblazoned with the Zen logo across the length of both sides.

Coop parked his Jeep around the side of the building, closer to the dental office across the parking area, and made his way to the entrance, which was locked and required members to use a keycard for access on weekends and non-business hours. As Coop was getting ready to call Joe's cell phone, a man came out the door, and Coop took advantage and stepped into the reception area.

He hung out at the main counter, listening to the soft ambient music drifting through the air. Within minutes, Joe came from around the corner. "Mr. Harrington?"

Coop nodded. "Yes, thanks for meeting me, Mr. Ward."

He delivered Coop an exasperated look. "As I told you when we talked, I'm in the midst of getting things set for Michelle's memorial tomorrow. I don't have much time to spare."

"You have my sincere condolences. Hopefully, it won't take long. Do you want to talk here or somewhere more private?"

Joe led him to a short hallway and a small alcove where there was a juice and coffee bar with a few tables and chairs. "We can sit in here. It's not open on Sundays."

Coop pulled out a chair at one of the small bistro-style tables. "I'm most interested in your thoughts and observations the night of the gala. Did Michelle mention being worried about anyone in particular or did she seem agitated?"

Joe shook his head. "No. No more so than usual. She wasn't thrilled that I was going to be late, but I had something to take care of here at Zen. I didn't really get involved in the political aspect. That was all Michelle."

"As I'm sure you know, when a wife is murdered, the husband is the first suspect. Did you have anything to do with your wife's murder?"

He smirked and shook his head. "No, I didn't. I never left the table and was nowhere near her when she was killed."

"I understand that, but that doesn't mean you weren't involved. You could have paid someone to kill her. You stand to inherit quite a bit, not to mention her million-dollar life insurance, and will walk away with a substantial financial gain."

"We each had life insurance policies to protect our business. I didn't hire anyone to kill my wife. That's an offensive accusation."

"Were you having an affair?"

"Absolutely not," said Joe. The lie rolled off his tongue with ease.

Coop pulled his cell phone from his pocket. It was cued up to the video Ross captured last night of Joe and Paula at his house. Coop hit play and watched Joe's swagger wilt. "How might you explain this?"

Joe's jaw tensed, and his eyes narrowed. "Okay, okay. Michelle and I had a non-traditional marriage. An open one. As long as we were discreet, we had an agreement when it came to other relationships."

"I see," said Coop, closing the screen on his phone. "So, Michelle had other men in her life?"

Joe shrugged. "I don't know. We had a don't ask don't tell policy."

"So, who do you think killed Michelle?"

"I'm sure one of the politicians she was always sparring with. She made a habit of stirring up trouble for them. Like I said, I wasn't involved in that part of Michelle's life. I have my hands full with running Zen."

"So, no theories on our part? Are you confident the police will find the killer? You don't seem that interested."

With a quick shrug of his shoulders, Joe stared at Coop. "I don't know. I mean how many murders go unsolved? Isn't it something like half? Look at the crap politicians get away with. That's what Michelle was fighting to change. She wanted nothing more than to expose them for what they really were. I admired her for that, but it wasn't my wheelhouse. I stayed out of all of it. It's probably what got her killed."

"How long have you been involved with Paula?"

"It just sort of happened over the last year or so, I guess. We've been working together quite a bit." Coop resisted the urge to reach across the table and wipe the smug look off Joe's face.

"You mentioned you have an open marriage. Do you and Paula have that same arrangement? Are you involved with other women?"

"We haven't discussed it, but no. I'm not involved with anyone else."

"My understanding is that Mr. Carlisle retains the controlling interest in Zen since Michelle signed her interest over to him when she decided to run for office. How do you see that working out for you?"

Anger and surprise flashed in Joe's eyes. He didn't know about that little wrinkle. The veins in his thick neck bulged, and Coop took delight in watching him squirm.

After several moments, Joe spoke, "I'm sure Mr. Carlisle will agree to sign them over to me. I'm not worried about it. He's been great so far, and I have no doubt he'll do the right thing by Michelle."

Coop slipped his phone back in his pocket and collected his notepad. "One last question, Mr. Ward. Are you familiar with the drug succinylcholine that was used to kill your wife? Since you have a clear motive, it's important to know if you had access to the murder weapon."

Joe's jaw tightened, and the veins were back on his neck. "I resent what you're suggesting."

Coop shrugged. "Like I said, the husband is the most likely suspect. So far, you've lied about your affair with Paula and clearly have a motive. It's a simple question and one I'm sure the police will be asking, too."

"The answer is no. When the police told me about it, they had to explain it to me. We don't use it here, and I had nothing to do with Michelle's death." He glanced at the clock. "I need to get back to work. I'll let you see yourself out."

Joe rose from his seat and without another word, trudged back in the direction of the reception desk, leaving Coop in the alcove.

By the time Coop reached the door, there was no sign of Joe. He left the building and walked to the Jeep, where he sat and perused his notes. He checked his watch and waited. Moments later, Madison texted that Paula was on the move.

Coop didn't have to wait long before Paula and her sporty little car pulled in front of Zen and parked next to Joe's truck. He predicted Joe would call her once Coop left to let her know the coast was clear.

By the time she collected her Yorkie and tote bag, Coop was at the front of her car. "Hey, Paula. I just got done talking to Joe." He extended his hand, and she stared at him, her head cocked in confusion. "I'm Cooper Harrington, a private detective investigating Michelle's death."

Her eyes widened, and she finally found her voice. "I'm in a bit of a hurry."

Coop smiled. "Understood. This will only take a minute. I just wanted to verify your whereabouts the night of the gala and Michelle's murder."

"I was here at work. I think I left around eight."

"So, Joe left before you?"

"Uh, yeah. He was in a hurry to meet Michelle."

"And how long have the two of you been involved romantically?"

She blinked her eyes repeatedly and swallowed hard. "We're not involved. We're just work colleagues."

Coop sighed. "Paula, Joe already confirmed your relationship, and I've got some video proof I shared with him."

Tears filled her eyes, and her face scrunched up, like she was about to shift into a full-blown cryfest. "I don't see what that has to do with anything."

"Well, it gives you both a motive to want Michelle dead. Did you have anything to do with her murder? Did you visit the gala that night?"

The fake crying morphed into anger. "No, I didn't go to the stupid gala. I left here and went home. I didn't have anything to do with Michelle's death."

"Can anyone vouch for your whereabouts here at Zen or at your house?"

She shook her head. "I was alone." Her little dog squirmed in her arms, and she glanced down at it. "I need to go. I don't appreciate you attacking me like this."

Coop stepped back. "Not attacking you, just asking questions and making the most of my trip down here to talk to Joe. Just happened to see you pull up and thought why not kill two birds with one stone, you know?"

"We're both very upset about Michelle and doing our best to honor her memory. If you'll excuse me, I need to get inside and help Joe with the rest of the setup for tomorrow."

"Sure, thanks for your time, Paula." Coop left her to deal with her dog and the door and hotfooted it back to his Jeep. As he walked, he couldn't help but think what two despicable human beings they were.

He checked the time and then slid his phone from his pocket. He tapped in the number for Helene Brooks.

She answered with a friendly voice, "Helene Brooks."

"Ms. Brooks, my name is Cooper Harrington, I'm a private detective looking into the death of Michelle Roberts at the gala you attended last weekend. I was hoping to set up a time to ask you a few questions."

"Oh, yes, that was horrific. I'm not sure how I can help but sure. I'm just on my way to the grocery store. I could meet you now, I guess." She mentioned a donut and coffee place he knew.

"That works. I'm only a few minutes away."

Coop turned the Jeep and headed in the direction of Dough and Joe. He approved of her choice of places to meet. He already liked this lady and hoped she wasn't involved.

When he walked into the busy shop, Coop scanned the tables but didn't see anyone who looked like the photo in Helene's background report. He got in line and ordered a cinnamon and sugar donut and a large coffee. He'd already had his one cup at home but without AB to supervise his intake, he opted to cheat.

As he took his order to a table, a woman walked through the door. Dressed in stretchy sweatpants and a Bluebird Café t-shirt, she looked older than her photo, but he recognized her from the file. "Ms. Brooks," he said with a smile. "I'm Cooper Harrington. Can I get you a coffee?"

She smiled and waved his offer away. "Oh, no. I'll grab my own. You go ahead and get a table."

He found a table tucked into a corner and took a seat. By the time she arrived, his donut was gone, and he'd wiped the crystals of sugar from his mouth. He stood as she arrived with a cup.

"Thanks so much for meeting me on a Sunday. I appreciate it."

"No bother. I was goin' to grab a coffee here anyway before I tackle my shoppin'."

She had a round face with full cheeks and a grandmotherly way about her. She was in her sixties, a little chunky, and her cheerful demeanor and sweet Southern drawl put Coop at ease. She wasn't the high-power lobbyist type he was used to seeing.

"I understand most of your clients are in the music industry, right?"

She nodded as she sipped. "All my clients. I've been in the business for decades."

"Did you know Michelle Roberts or interact with her at the gala?"

"I met her when she was in the Tennessee Assembly, but I didn't know her, just from my time visitin' with the legislators. She's always been very supportive of the industry to my clients. I didn't talk to her that night." Her smile faded. "Poor thing."

"And you lobby in Washington, D.C. as well as here in Nashville, correct?"

She nodded. "Yes, I do make a few trips up there, but I try to stay away from that place. I only go when there's a bill up that will impact my clients."

"From what I've learned, Michelle was a bit abrasive and made her share of enemies in the political realm. Is there anyone you remember from the gala who comes to mind as someone who was an enemy of hers?"

She frowned and took another sip. "I hate to even say this because I have no idea, but Randy Boone was spittin' mad about Michelle's release of that audio of him. I also think Marcus Ryle was none too happy to have her runnin' against him. Now, I'm not sayin' either of them would kill her, but they're the two who come to mind from that night."

Coop nodded and finished his coffee. "Thanks again for taking the time to meet me, Ms. Brooks."

"I'm sorry I couldn't be of more help." She smiled, and they walked out of the donut shop together, where she waved as she climbed into her car.

Coop circled back to the main street that led to Belle Meade. He hoped an afternoon off would help all the information he'd gathered percolate, and he'd wake up with a revelation that would solve the case.

Randy had a motive and the opportunity, but Coop's gut told him Joe did it. He just couldn't figure out how. After talking to Helene, he didn't see her as a viable suspect.

He was still thinking when he pulled the Jeep in front of Aunt Camille's property. Thank goodness for muscle memory since he'd been preoccupied on the entire drive.

Gus was waiting for him at the door and after a welcome home pet, Coop followed his nose to the kitchen, where the aroma of fresh baked lemon cake mingled with the pork in the slow cooker. Charlie and Camille were at the island counter, working on the crossword in the newspaper.

When they saw him, they both stood, ready to load up and head to Silverwood. Coop offered to drive, and Gus rode in the backseat with his dad. As he drove, he checked the rearview mirror and smiled when he saw Gus nestled up against Charlie, who grinned and had his arm around the furry dog.

"Hey Dad, I meant to ask you what your plans are for going back home? I found a continuing education class I need for my Florida license. It's not ideal timing, being in the summer at the end of June, but if you're still here, I thought you and Aunt Camille might want to go with me. We could drive, take Gus, stay at the condo, and you two could do some sightseeing while I'm in class. We can tack on a day or two to make it a mini vacation."

Camille squealed with delight, and Charlie's grin

widened. His dad leaned forward. "That sounds like a wonderful trip. I might even call Jack to see if they want to come and bring the kids to see all the amusement parks in Florida. If that works, it would be a good time for me to head back to Nevada. Since I hate flying, going with them would make it easier. If they opt to drive, I could ride back with them."

"That's a great idea, Dad." Coop took the turn for Silverwood.

Camille beamed as they turned into the parking area. "If they have time, they could even come and stay here for a few days. I've got plenty of room."

Charlie nodded. "I'll call Jack this week and see what works best for them."

Camille turned toward the backseat. "You just make sure you're back here in the fall, Charlie. We'll be lost without you."

Coop's heart swelled when he realized the true happiness that came with spending the afternoon surrounded by the beautiful gardens at Silverwood with the three people—yes he considered Gus a person—he loved more than anything in the world.

CHAPTER NINETEEN

Monday dawned and after a quick shower, Coop slipped on one of his favorite t-shirts. A dark-brown one lettered with I RUN ON COFFEE & SARCASM. It was early, and the house was quiet. He remembered to take a button-down shirt and jacket and carried the hanger while he urged Gus out the front door to the Jeep.

He was counting on Madison, Ross, and AB to do the heavy lifting at the celebration of life. He'd pushed Joe and Paula too hard yesterday and burned his bridge with them. He doubted they would let him get too close.

The first order of business was brewing coffee. Once Coop had his oversized mug filled and sweetened, he settled in behind his desk. Much to his dismay, he hadn't woken with the answer to Michelle's murder.

Last night, after Ross reported that Paula and Joe were back at his house, he'd given Ross the night off, so he could join them today and keep an eye on things at the celebration. Coop needed the extra set of eyes and ears.

Gus sprang from his chair and moments later, AB's voice

drifted from the kitchen. She and Gus carried on a long conversation before she appeared with a fresh cup of decaf for Coop and a steaming cup of tea for herself.

When Coop looked up, he noticed the black business suit she wore, with her hair styled in the soft waves she favored for special occasions. "Wow, you look like you're ready for a power meeting or court or something."

She sighed and took a seat in front of his desk. "I just thought I'd try to look as different as possible from the last time Paula saw me."

"Yeah, that's a good thing. I went a little over the top yesterday with Joe. He denied that he was having an affair until I shared the video Ross captured. I pressed the issue of him having an excellent financial and personal motive to kill his wife. Then, I waited for Paula to arrive and bombarded her in the parking lot before she had a chance to go in and talk to Joe. She also denied the affair and manufactured some fake tears when I caught her. They're both horrid."

"So, how could he do it if he never left the table?" AB sipped from her cup and glanced over at Gus.

"Part of me keeps thinking Paula helped him somehow. But she wasn't there. We've been through the list of cars and the video footage. There's nothing to suggest she was at the gala. Somebody had to help him."

AB shrugged. "Or we're barking up the wrong tree. I'm still not convinced Randy is innocent."

"Oh…" Coop's eyes widened. "I forgot to tell you. His wife called me Saturday night. I met her at a coffee place by Vanderbilt. She didn't want Randy to know. She's the opposite of Randy. Calm, cool, collected. Says she understands why we're looking at her, but that she had no access to the drug. She thinks it likely came from a smaller clinic or ambulance service, not a surgical environment since there are so many protocols for drugs in that setting. She gave me the information to check her alibi for the night of the gala."

Coop wrote down the security office from the university and the name of Elana's assistant who could provide a guest list of those in attendance at the fundraiser. AB took the sticky note and nodded. "I'll get on this right away."

As Coop brooded in his office, hoping to see the connection he was missing, AB came through the door. "Elana's alibi is good. The chief of security even went so far as to check the logs for the hospital, where Elana would've had to go to obtain succinylcholine, and she never badged into the hospital, just the building where her office is at the university. The fundraiser was held in the same building, and I was able to verify with five different people on the guest list that Elana was there until it ended, well after Michelle's body was found. I think she's in the clear."

Coop sighed. "I'm not surprised. She was very credible. As much as I despise Randy and his ilk, I don't see how he could have orchestrated this complex of a crime in less than twenty-four hours. The catalyst for his anger was Michelle's release of the audio on Friday night. I just don't see it working."

With a frown, AB nodded her agreement "Like you said, we're missing something."

While they lamented their lack of progress, Madison and Ross arrived. They also dressed professionally, ready for their work at the celebration of life. As the four of them discussed their approach, Coop suggested he remain outside and watch those who attend. He would slip inside and stay close to the entrance to monitor which of their suspected attended.

The other three would arrive separately and spread out,

keeping watch over the guests, paying special attention to Joe and Paula, along with Randy, Daniel, Emily, and Marcus, if they showed. AB had a file with the photos of the suspects from their list so Madison and Ross could familiarize themselves with them. Along with those suspects, she included photos of Michelle's ex-husband, daughter, stepsons, and former sister-in-law.

Coop handed out the earpieces they would use to communicate during the event. They helped each other hide the small radio transmitters and microphones under their jackets and then tested each to make sure the reception was adequate.

"If anything goes wrong with the devices, just use a group text, and we'll do it that way. I'm just hoping not to draw attention to us being on our phones during the event." Coop adjusted the back of Ross' jacket and pronounced him good to go.

Coop left first, an hour before the celebration was due to begin, and parked so he had a view of the entrance. Both Joe's truck and Paula's car were already parked in front of the entrance. Ross stayed in his vehicle to help keep watch on the arrivals, while Coop opted to stand outside on the sidewalk leading to the entrance, his phone to his ear as if on a call.

Several people trickled into the venue about thirty minutes later. Kate and Jimmy from Ben's division slipped in with a group of guests, neither of them making eye contact with Coop.

Anthony Carlisle and his wife, along with Eliza, Maxine, and Diane, were among the first guests to arrive who Coop recognized. Several other people made their way to the entrance, but none of them were on Coop's radar, and he didn't remember them from the gala.

Three black SUVs pulled into the lot and idled behind the cars already parked in front of the building. Daniel emerged from the back of one of them, along with Governor Brown. Several other people dressed in dark suits came from the other vehicles before the drivers left to park. Coop recognized a few as members of the legislature.

Coop walked down the sidewalk and around the end of the building, not wanting to draw attention to himself. While he was waiting for Governor Brown's entourage to file through the door, he spotted Emily Harper, followed by Jonathan Winters and his wife. Ross slipped through the door after them.

Arthur and Victoria Sinclair were among a group who arrived a few minutes before a limousine pulled up to the front of the building, and Barry, Poppy, and Bridget Marshall emerged from the back of it. Bridget looked even thinner than she had when they'd seen her at Poppy's house, her black dress hanging from her small frame. She walked between her dad and Poppy. Both held her arms, as if helping to support her.

With only five minutes before the event was due to start, right on cue, AB and Madison came from across the parking lot. They walked by Coop and didn't acknowledge him as they hurried through the door.

Coop slipped his phone back in his pocket and made his way to the door, where he found a line of people. They were all waiting to sign the guestbook stationed at the entrance of the double doors that led to the atrium. Instrumental music played in the background, and soft whispers of the guests filled the air.

Coop hung near the doorway, letting new arrivals cut in front of him. He still hadn't seen Marcus or Randy. He stepped away from the line and, in a low voice, spoke into his microphone, asking if anyone else had seen them.

All three responses were negative. Madison reported that she had eyes on Joe, who was seated in the front row of chairs, closest to where a podium was stationed, along with a huge photo of Michelle flanked by dozens of flower arrangements.

Ross was on the opposite side of the room, keeping his eye on Paula, who sat next to Joe. He added that a woman he didn't recognize sat next to Paula. He took a photo and sent it to the group.

AB reported that she was seated behind Barry Marshall and his family with a good view of Daniel and Emily.

Coop looked at the photo Ross sent, but he didn't recognize the woman either. The line dwindled and soon, Coop found himself at the entrance. As he slipped into a chair in the back of the room, the sound system buzzed, and Paula's voice greeted the guests.

She thanked everyone for coming to honor Michelle and reminded them there would be a luncheon for everyone on the patio after they all had a chance to share and remember Michelle.

Coop had a hard time stomaching her over-the-top tribute to Michelle. Paula waxed on about Michelle's vision and business acumen and her deep admiration for the woman who hired her to manage the flagship location. She ended with a tearful tribute and invited others to step forward to share their memories, while reminding them of how strong Michelle's poor husband had been in the face of such a tragic loss and mentioning Michelle's daughter Bridget.

Governor Brown was the first to step forward and praised Michelle's work ethic and focus on delivering for the people of Tennessee, saying how much he would miss working with her. Two legislators also stepped forward to express their admiration for Michelle and their time working with her in the legislature years ago.

Emily surprised Coop when she took the microphone. She gave a short, but eloquent, speech citing how she recognized Michelle was on the ballot running against her in the primary, but how they shared much of the same philosophies and principles when it came to holding government accountable and working for the people. She ended by saying not only had Michelle's family lost someone they loved, but the people of Tennessee lost a great voice and strong advocate, and Michelle would be sorely missed and fondly remembered.

Coop couldn't help but be impressed. She was beyond polished and came across as sincere and genuine. She would be raking in all the donor money that had been earmarked for Michelle. Marcus had missed an opportunity by choosing to skip the event.

After Anthony Carlisle and Diane said a few words and made sure Bridget knew they would be there for her as she navigated the loss of her mother, Joe finally took to the microphone to give his wife's eulogy. Despite having not appeared upset about Michelle's murder when Coop talked with him, he could barely choke out the words.

It was painful to watch, and Coop was convinced it was all an act.

As he wrapped up, talking about how much he would miss his wife and his adoration for her, he was overcome with sobs, and Paula rushed forward to put an arm around him.

Once he got to his seat, she returned to the microphone. "Joe put together a wonderful compilation of photos and memories. Please direct your attention to the screen."

Joe regained his composure long enough to start the video, and pictures of Michelle flashed across the screen. The guests watched the presentation while Coop and his team watched the guests.

When the video ended, Paula hurried back to the microphone. "We've got a lovely buffet setup for you on the patio, and our staff will be setting up some tables here in the atrium for those of you who would rather eat indoors, but there is lots of space outside, along with a complimentary bar. Please enjoy and remember to sign the guestbook for Joe. I also want to thank our wonderful staff for all they've done to put this event together today." She also pointed out where guests could find restrooms and invited them to tour the facility that had been Michelle's dream when she and Joe embarked on their business venture.

A few guests filtered outside, while others made their way to Joe to shake his hand and offer condolences before they made for the exit. As Governor Brown and his staff headed toward the exit, Coop noticed Maxine sought out Bridget and wrapped her in a long hug.

Coop stuck to the fringes of the crowd, avoiding Paula and Joe, and let Madison and Ross get closer, while he wandered outside. The long buffet tables were heaped with food from one of the popular local caterers.

Madison's voice came through Coop's earpiece. "I got in the receiving line and offered my condolences. The woman with Paula is her best friend Autumn Wells."

"Copy that," said Coop, adding her name to his notepad.

Guests were busy filling their plates, and Coop was eyeing a platter of chocolate chip cookies when AB's voice came through his earpiece. "Staff is moving the chairs and adding some tables in the atrium. Madison followed Joe and Paula out into the corridor. I'm going to stay here and keep an eye on the others."

Ross' voice added, "I'm going to get lost looking for the restroom and help Madison."

Several minutes went by before AB said, "Bridget just came through the double doors, crying and hysterical. She's with Poppy now, and Barry is on his phone. It looks like they're making their exit. The two of them are practically carrying her, and she is inconsolable."

Ross added, "Bridget ran past me in the hallway. She came from the other end."

Madison broadcasted next, her voice serious and clipped. "Just sent you a video I caught."

Coop retrieved his phone and shook his head. The video showed Joe and Paula, their arms wrapped around one another as they groped and kissed, clawing at each other's clothing in the doorway of one of the massage rooms at the end of the hallway.

The two of them had sunk even lower than Coop imagined. He was even more convinced of their involvement, or at least Joe's, in Michelle's death.

CHAPTER TWENTY

B y the time Coop reached the sidewalk outside Zen, the black limousine carrying the Marshall family was pulling out of the parking lot. Moments later, Coop's three colleagues joined him.

"Let's get out of here and meet back at the office," said Coop.

He made a stop at the Pickle Barrel and picked up lunch to take back to the office. By the time he arrived, the other three huddled around the conference room, with Gus relishing all the attention and treats he was collecting.

AB was on the laptop and glanced up when Coop deposited the takeout containers of sandwiches and salads on the table. "I'm digging into Paula's best friend to see what we can learn from her."

Coop dug into the beef dip he favored. "With the display Madison caught, I'm sure those two are up to their necks in Michelle's murder. They obviously think they've gotten away with it and don't even have the decency or humility to control themselves at Michelle's funeral. It's beyond belief."

Madison reached for a sandwich. "They were so wrapped up in their moment, they never saw me or Bridget. She was so quiet, I didn't notice her until I heard footsteps running away. Poor kid."

AB nibbled at her turkey gobbler. "She was already fragile and looked grief stricken. I'm sure seeing Joe all over Paula like that pushed her over the edge."

Ross finished his lunch and stood. "If you want me to keep an eye on them overnight, I'm going to head home and get some sleep."

Coop stared at the whiteboard behind Ross. "I was thinking of calling off the surveillance, but it might make sense to keep it up for a couple of days just to see what those two do now." He shrugged. "Go ahead and cover them tonight, and we can reevaluate tomorrow."

"Sounds good." Ross waved as he left the office.

Madison nodded. "I'll scoot back and keep an eye on Zen and follow if either of them leaves. I'll be in touch and let you know."

AB continued to eat while she tapped on the keyboard and focused on the screen of her laptop. As she read, she slapped her palm against the table. "Here's the link we've been missing. Autumn Wells is a veterinarian. She owns a clinic and practices in Bellevue."

Coop sighed. "Finally, a break. Now, we just need to figure out how to approach her without alerting Paula and Joe."

"An accessory to murder charge might trump her friendship."

"True," said Coop, staring at the laptop screen AB shared. "She's not married, has good credit, appears to be an upstanding citizen with not so much as a traffic ticket."

"Leads me to think, she may not actually be in on it.

Maybe they used her to get the drug without her knowledge?"

Coop shrugged. "Could be. Like Elana said, most doctors with a good reputation wouldn't risk prison and their career to provide a deadly drug to a murderer. Why don't you call her office and see if she's due back today."

AB scribbled the phone number on a sticky note. "Her home address is in Bellevue, too."

"Okay, let me think about the best approach." Coop took the opportunity to change and once back in his soft t-shirt, he felt better. He considered their next step as he paced the office while Gus watched him from his chair.

A few minutes later, AB came through the door. "The receptionist says she's out but due back by three o'clock."

Coop quit pacing and stood in front of Gus, petting his head. "Let's go pay her a visit at three o'clock and see what we learn. I'll call Ben when we get there and let him know we found a connection. If she's not involved, I think she'll be more than happy to make a statement to the police. If we get the idea she was involved, he'll be ready."

AB nodded and pointed at his shirt. "Makes me wish I would have thought ahead and brought a change of clothes."

He tapped his temple. "I'm always thinking, AB. You should know that by now." He grinned and went back to his computer to review the report on Dr. Autumn Wells before they set out for Bellevue.

———

Coop opted to take Gus, since they were visiting a veterinarian, and he would be great cover for them. When AB came out the back door, Gus moved from the passenger seat and wedged himself into the backseat. Normally, Gus wouldn't budge from his seat, but for AB, he made an exception.

Their route took them past Percy Warner Park, and Gus' tail went into hyperdrive. Coop glanced in the backseat. "Sorry, buddy. Next time. We've got a case to solve right now."

As he drove, Coop glanced over at AB. "I think we should take the approach that we believe Dr. Wells was used, not knowingly involved. I think we'll know right away if she turns defensive or if she tries to help, but if we accuse her first, she could get angry and defensive, and we'll get nowhere."

"Makes sense. I can't imagine someone with a successful career would be a party to murder. I don't care how good of a friend Paula is. I tend to think Dr. Wells was used."

He pulled in front of a grey house with white trim, surrounded by a large fenced yard and called Ben. After giving him a quick update and the address of Dr. Wells, Coop attached Gus' leash. The dog gave him a bit of side-eye. "I know, buddy. We're just pretending. It's not a real vet visit, okay? I just need you to act like you're sick."

The three of them stepped up to the porch, and AB opened the door, while Coop held onto Gus' leash. The woman at the reception desk smiled at them. "How can we help you?"

Coop pointed at Gus. "We're new to town and worried about Gus. He normally loves food and stopped eating yesterday. Hoping Dr. Wells could take a quick look at him."

Gus gave the woman his best puppy eyes and even added a little whine. She sighed. "Dr. Wells was out of the office today. We don't really have any appointments." She glanced at Gus, and he dropped his head while he stared at her. "Wait here, and I'll see if the doctor can spare a few minutes for you."

Moments later, she ushered them into an examination room and gave Coop a clipboard so he could fill out the new patient information.

After several minutes, a woman with a kind smile and deep-brown eyes that matched her hair came through the door. She bent down and held out her hand to Gus. "Aww, what a handsome boy. Mary tells me you're not feeling well."

She looked up at Coop and AB. "He stopped eating yesterday?"

Coop sighed. "I'm afraid we're here under false pretenses, Dr. Wells. I'm Cooper Harrington, and this is my associate Ms. Davenport. I'm a private detective, and we're investigating the murder of Michelle Roberts. The wife of Joe Ward from Zen."

AB added. "We're sorry to trick you, but we wanted to chat and didn't want to draw any unnecessary attention."

Dr. Wells frowned. "I don't understand. I mean I know about her murder. I didn't know her personally but am friends with Paula who manages Zen. I just attended the celebration of life today."

With a nod, Coop asked Gus to sit, and he and AB took their seats in the chairs against the wall. He gestured to the stool next to the examination table. "It's a bit of a story; you might want to take a seat."

Dr. Wells looked between them, wariness etched in her face, but she took a seat.

Coop cleared his throat. "I'm not sure if you know, but Michelle was murdered with succinylcholine."

Her eyes widened, and she shook her head. "No, I, uh, Paula said she was poisoned, and they thought it was some guy involved in the political party."

"We're here because we're concerned you may have been an unwitting party to the crime in that your clinic may have been used to obtain the succinylcholine."

She shook her head and panic rose in her eyes. "No, no, that can't be true."

AB caught the doctor's eye. "Has Joe Ward or Paula Kinkade ever visited here at the clinic?"

"Yes, as I said, Paula's a close friend." She sighed. "She told me that Joe and Michelle were getting divorced, and they had plans to marry once that was finalized."

AB nodded. "From what we know, that wasn't true. Paula and Joe have been having an affair. So, they've been to your clinic. When was the last time they were here?"

Dr. Wells swiveled on her stool and tapped the keys on a laptop on the counter. "Let's see, I saw Princess about four weeks ago in March."

"Both Joe and Paula came to that appointment?" Coop asked.

She nodded. "Yes, they were worried about her. It was right after I closed. They thought she ate an elastic hairband, so I told them to bring her out, and I'll check her."

"Can you show us where you treated the dog?"

With a nod, Dr. Wells stood. "Sure, it was in the main treatment area. I have a large open area where I do my procedures and other more invasive treatments." She gestured for them to follow her.

She led the way down the hall to a large room set up with portable metal tables and several treatment bays. Each bay had several cabinets and drawers, adjustable overhead lighting equipment, sinks, and counter space.

Dr. Wells gestured to the treatment bay on the end nearest a room with large windows. "I brought Princess here and ended up taking her in there," she pointed to the far end of the space, "for an x-ray to be sure."

"Did you have to administer any drugs to her?" asked Coop.

She nodded. "Yes, I had to give her an injection. I used a mild sedative to keep her still."

"Show me the steps you took. Where did you get the drug?"

Dr. Wells nodded and turned to the large upper cabinet in the treatment bay. She unlocked it and revealed shelves filled with a variety of vials and bottles. Coop stepped closer to get a better look. "Is succinylcholine stored in this same cabinet?"

She pointed at the shelf and nodded. "Yes, all the drugs are stored here." She shook her head and stared at the cabinet. "Normally, my tech would be with me and prepare the injection, but I was on my own."

"Were either of them here without you when the cabinet was open? Like when you took Princess to the x-ray room?"

Dr. Wells put her hand to her chest. "I remember after they left with Princess, I relocked the cabinet, but it was open while they were here. Paula came with me to the x-ray room, but Joe stayed out here."

AB looked around the space. "Was any of your staff here?"

Dr. Wells cocked her head. "No, we had closed, and they were gone. I was still here catching up on emails and stuff when Paula called."

Coop pointed at the shelf again. "Could you do an inventory on your supply of succinylcholine and see if any is missing?"

As the realization hit her, Dr. Wells paled. "Yes, yes. I'll do it right now." She went to another laptop on the counter and tapped a few keys. As she scrolled through screens, she mumbled and then turned to AB and Coop. "I printed out the inventory. I just need to go around and count what I have and see if it matches, but I've already got a sick feeling."

Coop and AB, along with Gus, who was sticking to Coop's leg like dog hair on Aunt Camille's velvet sofa, waited as Dr. Wells visited each treatment bay and unlocked the medicine cabinets. She then went to the surgical room and when she returned, she shook her head. "I'm missing one vial. I want to double check and recount, but the more I think about it, I'm certain what you're suggesting happened."

AB took a few steps toward Dr. Wells. "I'm happy to help you count."

Tears filled Dr. Wells' eyes. "Thanks, I'm just sick about this. I can't believe Paula would do this to me."

Coop settled into a chair near the doorway. "Did you find the elastic band in Princess?"

"No, nothing. She was fine." Dr. Wells shook her head. "Paula was so relieved, and they thanked me for staying late for them. She said one of the staff was missing the hairband, and Princess had been in the room, so they thought she must have eaten it." She hung her head. "I was duped. I'm sure of it now."

AB helped Dr. Wells, and they revisited each of the medicine storage cabinets and counted the vials. When they came from the operating room, AB caught Coop's eye and shook her head.

Dr. Wells leaned against the counter closest to where Coop and Gus waited. "Now what?" Her voice cracked. "I don't want to lose my license or my practice because of this, but I'm going to be in trouble."

Coop pulled out his cell phone. "One of my best friends is the chief of detectives for Nashville. Let's get him out here to take your statement and go from there. You're cooperating and didn't knowingly do anything wrong."

She sighed. "I was careless though and left the medicine cabinet unlocked. That'll go against me with the board."

"Try not to get ahead of yourself. Let's see what happens. I'm also a lawyer, so if you need representation, I'll do all I can for you." Coop smiled at her and pointed to his phone. "I'll give my friend a call right now."

With a long sigh, Dr. Wells nodded. "Okay. This is a nightmare."

———

It was close to the dinner hour by the time Coop and AB got back to the office, having left Dr. Wells in the hands of Ben and his team. Gus hurried inside and ran to his chair in Coop's office. He was done with adventures that involved veterinary clinics.

As Coop and AB discussed their next steps, which now that the police were involved and had a strong connection leading to Joe and Paula, might be moot, Coop's cell phone rang.

"Hey, Dad. What's up?"

"I'm at the hospital with Camille."

Coop's heart thudded in his chest. "I'll be right there."

"She's okay, don't panic. She was cutting fruit in the kitchen and sliced her hand. It's pretty deep. I just brought her to the ER for stitches. Wanted you to know."

"We're still at the office, but I'll be there in a few minutes."

He disconnected and met AB's eyes, filled with concern. "Aunt Camille cut her hand, and Dad took her to the ER. I'm going to run over there and check on them. Would you mind running Gus home for me?"

"Sure, no problem. You go, and I'll lock up here."

Coop was out the door in a flash and pulled into the ER parking lot within five minutes. He found his dad in the waiting room and hurried to him. "Dad, how is she?"

"They've got her in the back. Said she'll need a few stitches, but she's in good spirits. Upset at all the fuss."

Coop breathed out a long breath and slid into the seat next to his dad. "My heart almost stopped when you said she was at the hospital. I don't think I could handle anything happening to her. Or to you."

Charlie patted his son's arm. "She's a tough cookie and so am I. It's just a cut. She'll be fine."

As they sat there, Poppy and Barry rushed through the door, both of them pale, their faces drawn with worry and fear.

Coop's forehead creased. "I'll be right back, Dad. I know those two."

He walked over to them, where they were standing in line for the reception counter. "Mr. Marshall," he said, extending his hand. "Is there anything I can do to help you?"

Barry darted his eyes between Coop and his sister. "It's Bridget. She took a bunch of pills, and the ambulance just brought her in."

CHAPTER TWENTY-ONE

B arry gripped Coop's forearm. "She's been distraught since the celebration of life for Michelle."

Tears streamed down Poppy's cheeks. "It's my fault. I gave her a sleeping pill, hoping it would help her get some rest."

Barry shook his head. "It's not your fault, Poppy." He turned to Coop. "Bridget got the rest of the bottle from the bathroom and took them all."

"When I went in to check on her, I found the bottle on the floor next to her bed."

"I'm so sorry. AB and I were at the service and noticed how upset she was when you left."

Barry shook his head. "I don't understand any of this. Bridget barely spoke to Michelle, but ever since her death, she's been in a state. I shouldn't have let her go to the celebration. It was too much, I guess."

The receptionist called out to them, and they stepped forward. As Poppy explained they were there for Bridget, Coop lowered his voice and leaned closer to Barry, slipping his business card into his hand. "I may know more about what upset Bridget at the celebration. Right now, all that matters is her recovery, but when you're up to it, give me a call. My cell number is on the back."

Barry's forehead creased as he nodded. "I'll do that, Mr. Harrington. Thank you."

Moments later, they were whisked through the door and disappeared around the corner.

Since Coop was in line, he stepped forward to inquire about Camille. The receptionist said they were welcome to come back and sit with her. She was almost done. Coop motioned to Charlie, who hurried to join him.

Coop pointed to his phone. "I need to update AB and check in with her. She took Gus to the house. I'll be in as soon as I'm done with the call."

Charlie went through the door, and Coop stepped outside to call AB. She answered on the first ring. "Hey, AB. Just checking in. Aunt Camille is getting stitches. She's almost done. Dad is back there with her now."

"Oh, that's good news. I'm still at your house with Gus. Thought I'd clean up the kitchen and finish the fruit salad Camille was making."

"You're the best, AB. I'm not sure what I'd do without you."

She laughed. "Gus had his dinner and is resting after the trauma of his visit to the vet."

"Speaking of trauma. You'll never guess who I ran into in the ER waiting room."

"If it was Gerard Butler, I'll be right there."

He chuckled. AB did have a bit of an infatuation for the actor. "No, Barry and Poppy Marshall."

"What?"

"I know. They were there because Bridget was brought in by ambulance. She took an overdose of sleeping pills."

"Oh, no. That poor girl. It makes me want to punch that smug Joe right in the face. He and Paula are beyond awful."

"Yes, they are. I get why Bridget would be upset seeing Joe with Paula like that, but why would she want to kill herself?"

"Young girls don't always make sense, Coop."

"Yeah, I know, but it just seems like an overreaction. I think there's more to this. I told Barry we might have some insight into why Bridget was so upset at the service, and he could call me once Bridget was stable."

"Hopefully, she'll be okay."

"I hope so. They've been through enough."

"I'll hang out here until you guys get home. Dinner's basically ready. I'm keeping it warm."

"You're the best, AB. We'll see you soon."

He disconnected and walked back into the waiting room. As he stepped toward the reception counter, the door opened, and Charlie and Camille came through it, laughing and smiling.

"Oh, Coop, there you are. Your dad told me you were calling AB. He really shouldn't have bothered you. It was just a cut." She held up her bandaged left hand.

Coop put his arm around her shoulders and squeezed her tight. "Nonsense. I'm glad it was only a cut. AB is at the house, waiting on us."

As they walked to the parking lot, Coop texted AB to let her know they were on their way. While Coop's dad got behind the wheel, he helped his aunt get buckled in on the passenger side of her car. "I'll follow you guys to the house."

Coop's Jeep was parked a few spaces away, and he pulled in behind his dad. They were back at the house within a few minutes, and Coop rushed to help Aunt Camille from the car to the house.

AB had dinner on the table, complete with the offending

fruit salad that had sent Camille to the hospital. Despite her protests, everyone waited on Camille and made sure she was comfortable and had everything she needed before they dug into their own plates.

While they ate, Charlie reported that Jack was mulling over the idea of bringing his family to Florida for a visit during Coop's class. "He wasn't sure it would work out for them, but he was nice enough to volunteer to fly back himself and accompany me back home."

"That's nice of him," said Coop. "But if it doesn't work for a visit, I could fly back with you to Nevada. Or we could make a road trip. I need to be better about making time to visit him and my nieces and nephews."

Charlie smiled. "I know Jack would love that. We can talk about it later and figure out the logistics. I do want to get home after our Florida trip, one way or the other."

Camille put her fork down. "But Charlie promised he'd be back in the fall." She started to get up from her chair and winced. "If y'all don't mind, I think I'm going to call it a night. Thank you, AB, for rescuing dinner."

"Don't mention it. Thanks for having me," said AB. "Do you need some help getting ready for bed?"

Camille looked at her hand and shrugged. "I hate that I do, but I think I might."

AB put her napkin on the table and linked her arm in Camille's. "We'll get you settled, then I'll bring you some ice cream and a cookie for dessert."

"You're too good to me, AB." Camille chattered on as they walked toward her wing of the house.

Coop and Charlie were busy gathering the dishes from the table when his cell phone rang. He raised his brows at the name on his phone. "Mr. Marshall. How is Bridget?"

"They want to keep her overnight, but she's much better.

That's why I'm calling. I mentioned I ran into you in the waiting room. She asked that you and AB come to the hospital. She said it's important that she talk to you."

"Give me about twenty minutes, and we'll be there."

AB came into the kitchen as he disconnected. "That was Mr. Marshall. Bridget is stable and requested we come to talk with her."

"I promised Camille cookies and ice cream."

Charlie motioned for them to leave. "I'll handle the dishes and make sure Camille gets her dessert. You two go on."

AB collected her purse and slipped into the passenger seat of Coop's Jeep. They were back at the hospital in under twenty minutes and took the elevator to Bridget's floor. They made their way through the hall and stepped into the doorway of the dimly lit room.

Coop spotted Barry, who came to the door. "Thanks for coming so quickly. I appreciate it. Bridget is out of the woods. They want to monitor her tonight and have her talk to a psychologist, but she insists she needs to talk to the two of you tonight."

"Understood. We're happy to help."

Barry sighed. "I'm going to see if I can talk Poppy into going to the cafeteria to get some coffee while you're here."

"Sure," said Coop. "We can stay until you get back."

Barry nodded and stepped further into the room, disappearing behind the half-drawn curtain.

Moments later, he and Poppy came to the doorway, both looking older and more tired than they had when he'd seen them in the waiting room. Poppy smiled at them. "Thank you for coming. We appreciate it. We told her you were here."

Barry took her arm in his. "We'll just be in the cafeteria. You've got my cell number if you need us."

"No problem. Take your time," said Coop.

AB stepped across the room first and took the side nearest the window. "Hi, Bridget."

Coop glanced at Bridget's pale face, and her dark hair splayed across the white pillowcase. "Hey, Bridget. How are you feeling?"

The young woman sighed. "Foolish and embarrassed, mostly."

AB reached for her hand. "You'll feel better when you get home. We're just glad you're okay."

Tears leaked from Bridget's eyes. "I told Dad I wanted to talk to the two of you because I trust you. You were nice when you came to the house the day after my mom died. I noticed on your card, you're also a lawyer."

Coop nodded. "That's right."

"Can I hire you as my lawyer? I need to tell you something in confidence."

Coop met AB's eyes and then shrugged. "Sure, you can hire us, but you know we're working on behalf of Victoria and Arthur, so if there is a conflict, I won't be able to continue."

Bridget reached for the tray next to her bed. "Here's five dollars. Dad left his change here. I'm not worried about a conflict."

"Okay, it's official," said Coop, taking the five-dollar bill. "What can we do for you?"

She took a deep breath. "I know who killed my mom."

CHAPTER TWENTY-TWO

Coop and AB didn't interrupt and let Bridget, through tears, tell her story. Bridget explained she started going to Zen several months ago. She worked it into her school schedule and over the last few months Joe was there most of the times she was at the spa.

Joe helped her with the machines and weights in the gym and was always nice and glad to see her. His interest soon turned more flirtatious, and he would even slip into the massage room or sauna after she was done with her treatments.

As she described her interactions, the dinner Coop enjoyed a few hours ago felt like a knotted rope in his stomach.

"I hated Mom. I've hated her ever since the divorce. She never made time for me and always put her job first. She made more of an effort over this last year, but each time we had a plan, she found an excuse why she couldn't make it work. I just felt like nothing to her." Her voice cracked.

AB reached for the glass of water from the tray and held

it for her while Bridget sipped from the straw. "Thanks," she whispered. "Joe and I got to talking, and he felt much the same way. Mom put him last, too. He told me that he thought he'd made a mistake in marrying her, especially with her being older than he was. They had nothing in common."

Bridget hung her head. "Things escalated between us. We became more serious, and I looked forward to my time at the gym. It was like he really listened and cared about me." Tears fell from her eyes and leaked down her cheeks. "After what I saw today, I realize all of it was a lie."

Coop took advantage of the pause in her story and cleared his throat. "You were upset when you saw Joe and Paula together in the doorway today at your mom's memorial?"

Brittany nodded. "A few weeks ago, Joe said he wanted to be with me. He told me his marriage to Mom was over, and they were going to divorce soon. She only wanted to stay married through the election. He said he didn't want to wait and figured out a way we could live the life we deserved together. He said we could buy a place in Costa Rica. He had it all picked out."

She cleared her throat. "He said he had a plan and would share it soon, but we had to keep it a secret." She took another sip of water. "When I told him I was going to the gala, he got really excited and said that was our chance."

It took several minutes for her to tell the rest of the story, with Bridget pausing and breaking down several times. "Joe said he had the perfect drug we could use to kill Mom, and nobody would ever know. He said it left no trace, and she'd be dead within minutes. He knew he'd be a prime suspect, so he convinced me I had to be the one to inject her. He even had me practice on oranges when we were at Zen."

She described the drawers of syringes they had at the

Med Spa at Zen and how they'd use one of the treatment rooms after hours to practice her technique.

"Joe made sure he was late to the gala and had an alibi. Before he sat at the table, he left the syringe for me in the bathroom, under the sink. Our plan was to wait for her to leave the table and get her alone, or if that didn't happen, he would say I asked to talk to her alone and lure her away from the table. As it worked out, she left on her own.

"When Mom left, I followed her and saw her slip into the library. I went to the bathroom, the one closest to the Great Hall, put the syringe in my handbag, and followed her. She was more interested in the text on her phone than me, but it didn't matter. It was over. She was in the chair and not even paying attention. I bent over like I was going to whisper something to her and plunged the needle into her."

Bridget sobbed, and AB patted her back, urging her to take breaths.

Once she had a bit more water, she continued, "It was horrible. She dropped the champagne glass and just kept staring at me, but she couldn't move or talk. She didn't even blink. I went to the door, waited to make sure nobody was around, and slipped out. I went back to the bathroom, washed my hands, then joined the people from our table to play the game."

Coop sighed. "What did you do with the syringe?"

"Joe told me to take it back to Zen in Green Hills. I kept it in my bag and took it home. I have a locker at Zen, and Joe said he'd retrieve it and dispose of it at the Med Spa with all the other syringes. They have those special containers to collect them. He said nobody would even notice. I went there the next day and did as he said."

"Have you talked to Joe since the gala?" Coop asked.

She shook her head. "No, he said before that we needed

to stay away from each other, and he would reach out to me at Zen once it was safe. He didn't want to draw any attention to us." Her face contorted into a mixture of sadness and anger. "When I saw him kissing Paula today, I realized the whole thing had been a setup. He used me."

"How did you and Joe communicate? Texts or calls?"

She shook her head. "No, he said we couldn't leave a trace. He left notes in my locker at Zen, and I did the same."

"Did you keep those notes?"

Color bloomed across her cheeks as fresh tears spilled over them. "Yes, I have them in a notebook in my bedroom."

Coop glanced at AB, who had a look of disbelief on her face. He moved the box of tissues closer to Bridget. "Do you know where Joe got the succinylcholine?"

She shook her head as she wiped her nose. "No, he just said he had a friend and could get it from her."

"You mentioned you were pre-med, so you were aware of what the drug did, right?"

Bridget nodded. "I knew, but I'd never used it or anything like that. Just what I knew from the textbooks." She sobbed and said, "I'll never get that image of her out of my mind."

Coop sighed. "This is very serious, Bridget. I can tell you we found out today where Joe obtained the drug, and the police are involved. Chances are if he's confronted, he's going to shift all the blame to you. As you said, he set you up. As your attorney, I would advise you to speak with the police first. Tell them everything you've told us. Tell them the truth. It's your best chance for a reduced sentence."

Her eyes widened as fresh tears pooled in them.

He shook his head. "I'm not going to lie to you; you're going to be in trouble. With what you told us, the prosecutor may elect to charge you with something less than murder, but you're not going to walk away from this. The best you can do is lower your charge and make sure Joe pays in full for his part in this. I agree that you were manipulated, but it doesn't excuse your actions. I'll do my very best for you, and I can also recommend another attorney with more experience with murder cases, if it comes to a trial."

Bridget nodded as tears plopped onto the sheet across her chest. "I have to tell Dad and Poppy, first."

AB glanced toward the door. "We can stay here while you do that or let you talk to them on your own, whatever you want."

Coop stepped away from Bridget's bedside. "If you're in agreement, I'll contact my friend with the police and get him over here to get your statement now before Joe paints a different picture."

Bridget sighed, and a sob escaped from her mouth. "I don't have much choice, do I?" She reached for a tissue and blotted her face. "That's why I took the pills. I thought it would be easier if I just went to sleep and never woke up. Dad would never have to know, and it would be over."

"It's up to you, Bridget. I'm just giving you my best advice. Based on what you've said, Joe has been manipulating you from the start. I'm sure his plan is to implicate you to save himself. I'd suggest you turn the tables on that, tell the truth, and expose him for what he is. Granted, you'll pay too, but I think it's your best chance."

She closed her eyes for a few moments. "Okay, go ahead and call him. I'll talk to Dad and Poppy on my own. I need to face them at some point. Might as well be now."

The door to her room opened slowly, and Barry stepped into the room. "We're back. How's she doing?"

Coop gestured to the foot of the bed. "Bridget has something she needs to tell both of you. AB and I are going to step out into the waiting room at the end of the hall."

Poppy followed her brother and reached out to Coop as he walked by her. "Thanks again for coming."

"Sure, not a problem." His heart broke for what they were about to endure.

He and AB were silent on their trip to the waiting area. Coop took his phone out of his pocket. "I'm going to head outside to make this call to Ben. I don't need anyone eavesdropping."

AB shook her head. "This is a horrible situation. I didn't like Joe before, but this takes my disgust to a new level."

"Yeah, there are no good options for Bridget, and she's not exactly innocent, but I agree; Joe is despicable."

Coop left AB, took the elevator to the lobby, and hurried outside. He found a quiet spot near a tree and tapped the screen.

Moments later Ben answered. "Hey, Coop. Thanks for the tip on the veterinarian. She seems credible to us, and we're in the process of getting search warrants for Zen, along with Joe's house, Paula's house, and their vehicles."

"Well, I've got another wrinkle for you. You're going to want to come over to Vanderbilt and get a statement from Bridget Marshall. I'm her attorney as of about thirty minutes ago, and she agreed to have me contact you so she could explain how her mother was killed. You'll want to hear this before you serve your warrants."

"Whoa. Okay, that's a twist I didn't see coming. I'm leaving now and will bring Kate. See you in a few." He paused. "If you keep this up, I'm going to have to pay you a consultancy fee."

"I'll put it on your tab, big guy." Coop disconnected and trudged back inside the building.

He could only imagine what Barry and Poppy were

enduring as Bridget explained what she'd done. His heart ached for them.

———

Before Ben arrived, Barry talked to Coop in the hallway and wanted him to know he would cover all of Bridget's legal expenses, and he made it clear that no expense was to be spared when it came to keeping his little girl from going to prison. Coop assured him he would do his best but wanted him to prepare himself for some kind of jail time. He explained that the premeditation part of this crime could qualify as a first-degree murder charge. The best they might hope for is voluntary manslaughter, which carried a minimum penalty of three years.

Coop hated to see the absolute devastation in Barry's eyes, but he wanted him prepared.

With the police involved, Coop called off Madison and Ross and let them know the case was all but closed. Then, he sent AB home in a taxi to get some rest while he sat with Bridget as she told her story to Ben and Kate. They, like Coop, didn't react and maintained a professional demeanor, asking questions and getting as many details from Bridget as possible.

By the time they wrapped up with the detectives, Bridget was exhausted and needed her rest. Coop said goodbye to Ben and Kate at the elevator and met Poppy and Barry in the waiting room.

The strain in their faces was even more profound than when he saw them earlier in the evening. "Bridget is tired, and the nurse just came in to check on her. She needs her rest. It's been a long few hours."

They stood, Barry with his hand around Poppy's shoulder. "What's going to happen to her?"

"It will be up to the prosecutor's office, but I'll do my best to get her the minimum charge. Telling the truth and getting in front of it, especially before Joe could twist the story, is important. I really can't say much, since Bridget is an adult and my client, even though you're paying the bill, Mr. Marshall."

"I understand and appreciate your position. I'm just so upset with Joe." Anger flashed in Barry's eyes, followed by immense sorrow. "I can't believe this is even happening. I feel like I failed her. I should have seen something was wrong."

Poppy shook her head. "We've been sitting here blaming ourselves for this all night. I just can't imagine her agreeing to his harebrained idea."

"It's hard to understand, and she was clearly distraught about all of it, especially once she figured out Joe was manipulating her. I'm just glad she spoke up when she did. I'm sorry you have to go through this. Try to get some rest, and we'll know more tomorrow, I'm sure."

He urged them downstairs, and they took the elevator together. He left them in the parking garage and promised to talk with them tomorrow.

Filled with despair and completely exhausted, Coop drove home, parked the Jeep, and made his way through the quiet house to his bedroom. He sank into his pillow, thankful he wasn't in Barry's position, willing his mind to quiet. Moments later, Gus moved from his sleeping spot on his chair and put his nose right next to Coop's head.

"Hey, sorry I woke you, buddy," said Coop, reaching out to him.

Gus hopped up on the bed and curled next to him. Coop

smiled and rested his hand in the warm fur of his belly. Gus rarely slept with Coop, but he had a knack for sensing stress and was always there to comfort Coop. As he felt the steady beat of Gus' heart next to him, Coop closed his eyes and drifted off, anxious to escape the sadness of the day.

CHAPTER TWENTY-THREE

Coop woke to the sound of birds chirping and sunlight coming through the windows, where he'd forgotten to close his blinds. He was both anxious and filled with dread about what the day would bring after Bridget's confession.

He understood, better than most, how Bridget felt toward Michelle. He knew the heartbreak of being abandoned and feeling like she was less than nothing in the eyes of her mother. As much as Marlene irritated him, he'd never contemplated killing her. Thankfully, he'd had the stability and love from his dad, along with Uncle John and Aunt Camille, not to mention the close friends he'd found in Ben and AB. His life would have been very different without their steady guidance, support, and loyal friendship.

Bridget had access to money and anything she desired, but it was clear what she wanted most was the attention and love of her mother. As AB said, children always craved that, even from rotten parents. He understood the dysfunction that went with that desire.

After a shower and a cup of coffee with Camille, who was

trying to deal with her bandaged hand, and his dad, who was happy to turn the tables on Camille and help her, Coop and Gus headed to the Sinclairs to give them the latest news.

He'd called ahead, and Victoria met him at the door and led him and Gus to the patio where she had a table set up for them near the pool.

Coop situated Gus behind him, in the shade, and one of Victoria's staff delivered a stainless-steel bowl of water for him, while another brought iced teas to the table. Arthur hurried out of the house, apologizing as he took a seat. "Nice to see you, Mr. Harrington. Victoria tells me you have news."

"Yes, sad news, I'm afraid. The police are involved now and developing their case, so this information needs to stay just between us."

Both of them nodded. "Of course," said Victoria. "We haven't breathed a word about any of this ghastly business. We just want to put it behind us."

Coop took a long swallow of his sweet tea. "You'll be relieved to know it wasn't any of your guests associated with politics or the fundraiser."

Victoria smiled and reached for Arthur's hand. "That is good news."

"We discovered Joe, Michelle's husband, orchestrated the murder. He used Michelle's own daughter, Bridget, to carry it out, but he was the mastermind behind it."

Victoria gasped and turned pale. "Oh, that's awful. I'm sick for Barry and Poppy."

Arthur shook his head. "They've got to be devastated. What will happen to Bridget?"

"I don't know. I'm helping her as much as possible, but it will be up to the prosecutor as far as charges go."

Tears filled Victoria's eyes. "This is not what I expected." She brought her hand to her chest. "My heart is broken for the Marshall family. Please let Barry know we're on hand and happy to help if we can."

Coop finished his tea and nodded. "I will do that. I'm not at liberty to divulge much more due to Bridget asking us to represent her, but when I'm able, I'll get in touch and tell you more. Right now, we're just waiting for the police to finish their investigation and file the charges."

Arthur stood and reached inside his jacket pocket. He handed Coop a check. "We appreciate all your hard work. Having this wrapped up in just over a week is more than we expected."

Coop shook Arthur's hand. "That's kind of you, but we can just send you an invoice for anything outstanding."

Arthur shook his head. "You deserve a bonus. We know how seriously you took this case and the long hours you've put in. Just enjoy it. Take a vacation."

Coop thanked him and slipped it in his pocket without looking at the amount. He collected Gus, and Victoria showed them to a gate leading to a walkway connected to the driveway. "Thanks again for everything. I hope things work out for Bridget."

"Me too, Mrs. Sinclair."

———

As much as Coop understood what Bridget did was criminal and wrong, he couldn't shake the vision of her in prison. He wasn't sure she'd survive.

As he drove down the driveway, he put a call into Barry.

"Mr. Harrington, any news?"

"Nothing new, I'm afraid. I just left Victoria and Arthur. They wanted me to pass on their best to you and offered any help you needed."

"That was kind of them." He sighed, and his voice sounded weak. "Unless they have a time machine, I'm not sure what they could do."

"Have the doctors discussed an in-depth psychiatric evaluation for Bridget? I ask because it could help in her sentencing."

"Yes, Bridget called this morning and said the doctor would like her to undergo an evaluation, now that the drugs are out of her system, and she's stable from that. She's embarrassed and reluctant of course, but I encouraged her to just stay in the hospital for it. They have a behavioral health facility across the street. They're going to transfer her today, and she'll be there for a few days."

"I know this is tough, Barry. I'm sure you want her home, and I'm sure she'd rather be home. Hopefully, they'll help her, and the evaluation could help her case. The more she can do to show she's getting help, the better."

"I understand and from what I know, she isn't allowed visitors during this initial period. I'll keep you posted."

"Sounds good and if you need anything, just give me a call. Tell Bridget we're thinking of her."

"I appreciate that. I really do. Thank goodness for Poppy and the boys. I'm not sure I could make it through this without them. They're all here at the house with me now."

"Good, good. Family is most important right now. Take care, and I'll talk to you soon."

Coop disconnected as he pulled into the lot behind his office. When Coop and Gus came through the back door, they found AB at her desk, looking more like herself in jeans and a blouse. "So," she said, as Coop sat on the couch near her desk. "Have you heard from Ben yet?"

He shook his head while Gus hopped up next to him.

"No, I'm sure they're talking to the prosecutor and working on Joe. I'd love to see what he has to say."

Coop massaged the bottoms of Gus' paws while he talked, and Gus sprawled out and closed his eyes. "I'm certain they'll offer Bridget some sort of plea deal. She won't want to go through a trial. I'm not sure the gravity of it has sunk in for Barry and Poppy yet. He's hoping she won't have to go to prison. I tried to prepare them that it's a likely outcome, but I think they're in denial."

"All I can say is that Joe better get the book thrown at him. He saw Bridget's weakness and preyed upon her. He's lower than scum."

"Agreed," said Coop. "I'd love to watch his interrogation."

As they were talking, Coop's cell rang. "Hey, Ben."

"Just wanted to call and give you the latest. We executed the search warrants, and I've got the lab going through all the sharp containers at Zen, looking for the syringe that was used on Michelle. Paula cracked the moment we started asking questions. Threw Joe under the bus, saying it was his idea to use Dr. Wells and gain access to succinylcholine. She's singing like the proverbial bird, hoping to avoid jail."

"What about Joe?"

"He's playing dumb at the moment, but we're going to hit him harder with the statement from Dr. Wells, along with Paula's revelations and those of Bridget, of course. We've got Joe and Paula's phone and text records, which clearly show more than a professional relationship. No mention of the murder or the gala though."

"Did you get the handwritten notes Bridget kept?"

"Yeah, we collected those late last night. They'll come in handy. She also kept the brochures Joe gave her for a place in Costa Rica." Ben shook his head. "You know what's funny? He gave Paula the same song and dance. Promised her when everything settled down, they'd sell Zen and everything else and take the money and move to Costa Rica."

"Wow, he's something else. He must be more charming than he was when I talked with him."

"Yeah, it doesn't make sense to me," said Ben.

"Any news from the prosecutor's office on a plea deal for Bridget."

"Nothing official, but they're leaning toward voluntary manslaughter provided they can get Joe. She's been cooperative, and everything she's provided has been truthful from what I can tell. I think she's got a good shot at avoiding a murder charge."

"I hope so." Coop sighed. "I think she'd be much more sympathetic to a jury than Joe would."

"No doubt. He definitely used her and orchestrated the event. Took advantage of her. Not to say she's not responsible and could have said no, which is why she can't get off without facing time."

"I understand. It's hard to imagine her in prison. She's fragile."

"Get her a psych eval. That may help."

"Already in the works. Just talked to her dad, and they're moving her over to the behavioral unit for an evaluation. She'll be out of reach for a few days."

"Got it. I'll be in touch when I know anything more."

Coop put his phone in his pocket and remembered the check from Mr. Sinclair. He opened it, blinked as he took in the number of zeros on the check, and handed it to AB. "Wow," she said. "That's way more than they owe us."

"Arthur said we deserved it and to take a vacation."

"I knew I liked those two," said AB, opening the ledger to record it.

"Be sure to give Madison and Ross a little bonus for their

efforts. They put in some long days. And add a bonus onto your check."

She smiled. "Thanks, Coop. That's generous."

"Did you get my email about that class I signed up for in Florida in June?"

"Oh, yeah. I saw that. Meant to ask you, but we've been so busy, I forgot."

"Can you book the condo for the week before and the week after? I'm not certain yet, but Dad asked Jack about coming out with the kids to visit, so I just want to make sure we have space booked. Once I firm up dates with him, you can make plans to go down whenever they won't be there and take some time to soak up that Florida sunshine and lay on the beach for a week."

"Really? I would love that." She grinned and stomped her feet on the floor. "I can't wait."

"We're going to drive down, and then Dad is going back to Nevada with Jack. They're still figuring out if it will be Jack or the whole family coming and if he'll fly or drive, but he'll have somebody to help him if he flies."

"Oh, that's a great idea." She looked at the calendar on her screen. "What about the office?"

"We'll just close it for a week if it works out that we're both gone at the same time."

"Best idea ever. I'll get the condo reserved and get things organized."

"I'm getting hungry. I'll run and get us some lunch."

———

As soon as they sat down to pulled pork sandwiches and all the fixings, Ben called. Coop wiped the sauce from his fingers and hit the button. "You're on speaker with AB, Ben. You caught us at lunch."

"I just called to see if you two had time to swing by my office. We're interviewing Joe in about thirty minutes. I'll have the feed up on the television in my office. Just stay in there, and you can watch it. It's not exactly kosher, but we wouldn't have gotten this far without you."

"We'll be there and keep it to ourselves."

"If anybody asks, just say you're waiting for me. Can't help it if I'm absent-minded and forgot to close out the feed, right?" He chuckled.

"Got it. We'll be in your office."

They hurried and ate the rest of their lunch, locked the office, forwarded the phone to AB's cell, and loaded Gus in the Jeep. Coop broke the speed limit and got them to Ben's office with two minutes to spare.

The receptionist looked up from her computer. "Hey, Coop. Chief Mason said you'd be by to see him and could wait in his office." She buzzed them through with a smile and a dog treat for Gus.

The lights were off in Ben's office, and the blinds closed, but the door was unlocked. They slipped inside and closed the door behind them. Gus rushed to the corner behind Ben's desk and settled into the dog bed Ben kept for his favorite furry visitor.

Coop and AB moved the chairs in front of Ben's desk so they had a better view of the television screen and watched as Kate and Ben entered the interview room. Joe sat slumped in the chair, the same smug look on his face Coop remembered.

Gus stared at the screen, filled with Joe's image, and let out a low growl. Coop went over to him and petted him.

"Good boy, Gus. You're an excellent judge when it comes to humans."

He glanced up at AB. "We should have taken Gus to the gala. He would have picked out the culprit without a problem."

AB chuckled. "I think you're onto something. Instead of a dog whisperer, he's our criminal whisperer."

Kate's voice came from the speakers. She stated the names of the detectives present, along with the date and time, and reminded Joe of his rights he'd been read earlier. He again declined an attorney. "Innocent men don't need an attorney." He smirked as he addressed her.

"Fine, let's talk about your visit to Bellevue Veterinary Clinic and Dr. Wells in March of this year. Do you recall your visit there with a Yorkie named Princess, owned by Paula Kinkade?"

He nodded. "Yes, Paula thought she swallowed an elastic band. She's always dramatic when it comes to her dog."

"While you were there, did you take a vial of succinylcholine from the drugs cabinet in the treatment room?"

He scrunched up his face. "No, I wouldn't even know what it was."

"Would it surprise you to know that we have a statement from Paula Kinkade saying exactly that. She was with you, and you directed her to distract Dr. Wells so you could gain access to the drug. She further stated that the idea to dupe Dr. Wells was yours. The dog hadn't swallowed anything, but you asked her to call her friend, Dr. Wells, after hours and request an emergency visit for Princess."

He shook his head. "That's not what I remember. Paula was out of her mind, thinking the dog swallowed the elastic, and made me go with her to see the vet. That's it."

"So, you never took the succinylcholine from Dr. Wells' drug cabinet that she unlocked during the treatment of Princess? To be specific, the cabinet that was unlocked while you were left alone in the treatment bay, and she and Paula took the dog for an x-ray." She put a photo of the cabinet in the treatment bay in front of him. "For the purpose of the tape, I'm showing Mr. Ward a photo of the drug cabinet at Bellevue Veterinary Clinic."

"Nope."

Kate flipped a page in the file she had in front of her. "You said before that you didn't know what succinylcholine was until we told you about it being used in your wife's murder. Do you stand by that statement?"

"Yes."

"You also said you'd never used it or procured it for the purpose of killing your wife. Is that correct?"

"Yes, I've answered that already."

"Did you devise a plan to kill your wife with succinylcholine at the gala at the Sinclair Chateau and suggest that to her daughter, Bridget Marshall?"

Coop noticed Joe's eyes widen, but he kept up his bluster. He grimaced. "Her daughter is messed up. If she's saying that, she's lying. I did no such thing."

"Did you visit the bathroom in the hallway where the library and music room are located at the Sinclair Chateau on the night of the gala, prior to you joining your wife at her table?"

He darted his eyes upward. "Uh, yeah, I did. Needed to visit the little boys room before I sat down."

"Did you load a syringe with succinylcholine and leave it for Bridget in the bathroom, under the sink, at the Sinclair Chateau on the night of the gala?"

His forehead scrunched in disbelief, but Coop noticed the

veins in his neck bulge. "No, I didn't. This is quite the story Bridget told you. A load of absolute BS."

Ben glanced at a paper in the file he was holding. "Did you retrieve a syringe from Bridget's locker at Zen on Sunday, the day after the gala, and dispose of it in a sharps container in the Med Spa?"

The color rose from Joe's neck, and he reached for the cup of water in front of him. After taking a long swallow, he said, "No, I did not."

Kate flipped through the pages in the folder in front of her. "Going back to my earlier question about your trip to the Bellevue Veterinary Clinic. How do you explain your fingerprint on the inside of the drug cabinet at Bellevue Veterinary Clinic?"

He stared at Kate, his eyes narrowed and full of hatred.

AB whispered to Coop, "This is so much fun. It's like watching a sparring match. Kate and Ben are doing a good job of keeping him off guard."

Kate turned to another page. "Our lab went through all the sharps containers at the MedSpa and found a syringe with succinylcholine still in it. Your fingerprints are on that syringe, Mr. Ward. How do you explain that?"

His entire face turned beet red, and he clenched his fists atop the table.

"Further, Mr. Ward, we've obtained handwritten notes you left for Bridget in her locker at Zen. They are quite revealing and suggest you did indeed orchestrate a plan to murder your wife, instructing her on specifics. You promised her you'd have the life you both deserved and all the money you needed to move away and live in Costa Rica. She kept the brochures and printouts you gave her of the house you were going to buy."

Joe was silent for a few minutes, his fists tightening.

Kate and Ben said nothing.

Coop looked at AB and grinned. "They've got the jackal."

Joe stared at them from across the table. "I think I'd like to call a lawyer now."

She glanced over at Ben. "Hmm, boss, I seem to remember someone saying innocent men don't need a lawyer. Makes me think our guy might be guilty."

Ben grinned at her and then stared at Joe. "A lawyer is a fine idea. Best one you've had today, I'd say."

Kate smiled. "Joe Ward, I'm arresting you for conspiracy to commit premeditated first-degree murder of your wife Michelle Roberts." She winked at him. "Stay tuned for more charges. I'm just getting warmed up, but we'll let you call your lawyer so he can explain them in detail."

The smugness vanished from Joe's face. Coop pointed at the screen when he noticed tears slipping down his cheeks. "The cowards always cry," he said, turning to AB.

CHAPTER TWENTY-FOUR

Coop and AB continued to watch the screen, taking great delight in Kate slipping the cuffs behind Joe's back as he continued to cry and beg. A uniformed officer escorted him from the room. Kate turned off the recording, and the screen went blank.

Coop plucked two dog treats from the bag Ben kept on top of the file cabinet in the corner and rewarded Gus. A few minutes later, Ben came into his office, grinning from ear to ear. "Enjoy the show?"

"Oh, yes. Made our day, didn't it, AB?"

She nodded. "Big tough scumbag and then cries like a baby when he's caught."

"Like most of the worst of the worst. We've got him wrapped up tight. The DA is happy and has a few more charges to add to the sheet. He's agreed to voluntary manslaughter for Bridget and will recommend the minimum sentence. Three years."

AB sucked in a long breath. "That's going to be tough enough."

"They're going to get her into the minimum-security section over at the Deborah K. Johnson Rehabilitation Center. They have some good programs, and it's well run. It's the best we can do. She could be out in a year and serve the rest under probation. She'll just have to behave."

"I'm sure she'll behave," said Coop. "I just hope she can handle it mentally."

"I'm just glad we've got this arrogant son of a..." He glanced at AB. "Biscuit, locked up. He's not going to wiggle out of it."

Coop drummed his fingers on the top of Ben's desk. "How did you get the syringe evidence so quickly? I figured that would take days."

Ben winked. "Well, the lab thought it would be one of the larger syringes, just based on an almost full vial of the drug being stolen and the levels found in Michelle's urine, so they opted to check the largest capacity ones first. Most of the syringes were small, but there were only a handful of the large ones, and they hit paydirt right away. That was the piece we needed."

"That's fantastic," said AB.

Coop nodded his agreement. "I'll let Mr. Marshall know. He'll be relieved to know Joe is behind bars and facing a long sentence."

Ben's desk phone rang and he saluted Coop and AB. "Thanks again you two. You made our job much easier. Appreciate the help."

He picked up the phone, and Coop gestured for Gus to follow them. Once they were loaded into the Jeep, he left the parking lot. When he took a different turn from the one that led back to the office, AB gave him a quizzical look.

"I think we deserve a treat after all that."

He turned again and pulled into the lot next to Steve's Ice

Cream. AB waited with Gus on the swinging bench outside. Coop returned with two waffle cones, overflowing with Steve's homemade ice cream. He handed AB the strawberry and sat next to her with his coffee fudge.

He held out a small pup cup filled with whipped cream for Gus, who was happy to lick it clean. Coop and AB both moaned as they took their first bites. "Delicious. Thanks, Coop," said AB, taking another bite.

"I could treat you to ice cream each day, and it would never be enough to repay you for all you do for me. I truly appreciate you, AB. I know I don't say it often enough, but between everything you do at the office, not to mention helping me clean up my room, and dealing with my very trying mother... I'm not sure I could make it without you."

She cocked her head and grinned. "Why, Coop, that's so nice of you. I really don't mind. I love my job and spending time with you and Camille and your dad, it's the cherry on top."

"Ice cream isn't quite the vacation Mr. Sinclair suggested, but hopefully, it will tide you over until you get to Florida. It's not the best time of year being summer. We should try to plan something in the winter next time."

AB rested against the back of the wooden swing. "Anytime in Florida is the best time."

"We'll just have to make sure not to take on any tough cases between now and then. I wouldn't mind a little bit of our boring corporate work. This case was a tough one. It didn't end as happy as I hoped."

She took another bite. "Too many lies and secrets."

Coop chuckled. "And that's not counting the politicians."

"Heartbreaking, too," said AB, dabbing her lips with a napkin.

"That's why we're having ice cream. It makes everything better."

AB laughed. "You sound like your dad now."

"I'll take that as a compliment," said Coop, glancing down at Gus, licking cream from his mouth. "Don't tell them we stopped for ice cream without them."

With a grin, AB pulled her fingers across her mouth like a zipper. "Your secret is safe with me."

Coop took a bite of his cone and let the delicious blend of coffee and chocolate linger on his tongue. Over time, he'd learn he couldn't fix everything, but it didn't make it any easier.

He thought of Marlene in jail. He made a mental note to deposit money into her commissary account each week. She didn't deserve it, but he would give her that bit of grace.

It was a gorgeous spring day and instead of thinking about his latest client and what she faced, he chose to enjoy the colorful flowers in the planters along the sidewalk, the warmth of his good friend next to him, the deep-brown eyes of his faithful companion staring at him and begging for a bite of his cone, and the anticipation of spending some time in Florida with the people he loved most.

EPILOGUE

Deadly Deception is the fifth book in the Cooper Harrington Detective Novels. You'll discover a new case in each book in the series, but the characters you've come to know will continue throughout the series. Tammy plans to continue this series until she runs out of cases for Coop. The books don't have to be read in order but are more enjoyable when you do, since you'll learn more about Coop's backstory as the series unfolds. If you're a new reader to Coop's books, you won't want to miss the other novels in the series.

If you've missed reading any, here are the links to the entire series, in order.

Killer Music
Deadly Connection
Dead Wrong
Cold Killer
Deadly Deception

ACKNOWLEDGMENTS

Whenever I write a new mystery, I realize how much I love spending time with Coop, AB, Gus, and Aunt Camille. Along with the twisty mystery plot I love crafting, writing this series always feels like visiting old friends. I feel that way about the characters in my Hometown Harbor Series as well. I miss the characters when I have to be away from them and work on other projects.

My favorite part of writing fiction is character creation, and this book gave me some great opportunities. Originally, I didn't plan to have Coop's dad stay in Nashville so long, but I love having his character on hand to keep Aunt Camille company. Along with the regular cast, this story has a ton of interesting characters with plenty of motives for murder. Coop's mom also pops up in this story, which always makes things interesting for Coop.

As always, I'm thankful for my early readers, who are diligent when it comes to reading my manuscripts. My dad is still my greatest source of expertise in all things crime, being in law enforcement for over thirty years. We had several conversations about the "what if" questions that always fuel these books. I spent much of my career involved in the legislative branch of government and drew on those experiences to fuel the political aspects in this one.

Interesting fact, during my tenure in government, we had a constitutional officer murdered with succinylcholine. It was a strange case with her husband convicted and still in prison today. It is a unique method and almost the perfect weapon.

Thanks go to Elizabeth Mackey Graphic Design for my latest cover. She is beyond talented and never disappoints. Gus posing for these covers always makes me smile. Many thanks to my editor, Susan, for helping me polish the story.

I'm grateful for the support and encouragement of my friends and family as I continue to pursue my dream of writing. I appreciate all the readers who have taken the time to provide a review on Amazon, BookBub, or Goodreads. These reviews are especially important in promoting future books, so if you enjoy my novels, please consider leaving a review. I also encourage you to follow me on Amazon, and you'll be the first to know about new releases.

Remember to visit my website at www.tammylgrace.com or follow me on Facebook at www.facebook.com/tammylgrace. books to keep in touch—I'd love to hear from you.

MORE FROM TAMMY L. GRACE

GLASS BEACH COTTAGE SERIES

Beach Haven

Moonlight Beach

Beach Dreams

WRITING AS CASEY WILSON

A Dog's Hope

A Dog's Chance

WISHING TREE SERIES

The Wishing Tree

Wish Again

Overdue Wishes

SISTERS OF THE HEART SERIES

Greetings from Lavender Valley

Pathway to Lavender Valley

Sanctuary at Lavender Valley

Blossoms at Lavender Valley

Comfort in Lavender Valley

Reunion in Lavender Valley

Remember to subscribe to Tammy's exclusive group of readers for your gift, only available to readers on her mailing list. **Sign up at www.tammylgrace.com. Follow this link to subscribe at https://wp.me/P9umIy-e** and you'll receive the exclusive interview she did with all the canine characters in her Hometown Harbor Series.

Follow Tammy on Facebook by liking her page. You may also follow Tammy on book retailers or at BookBub by clicking on the follow button.

FROM THE AUTHOR

Thank you for reading the fifth book in the Cooper Harrington Detective Series. These mystery books are designed to be stand-alone reads, but I recommend reading them in order, as you'll learn more about the recurring characters. If you enjoyed it and are a fan of women's fiction, you'll want to try my HOMETOWN HARBOR SERIES or my GLASS BEACH COTTAGE SERIES or my newest series, SISTERS OF THE HEART. You can even start this one by downloading the first book, GREETINGS FROM LAVENDER VALLEY, for FREE!

The two books I've written as Casey Wilson, A DOG'S HOPE and A DOG'S CHANCE, both have received enthusiastic support from my readers and, if you're a dog lover, are must reads.

If you enjoy holiday stories, be sure to check out my CHRISTMAS IN SILVER FALLS SERIES and HOMETOWN CHRISTMAS SERIES. They are small-town Christmas stories of hope, friendship, and family. I'm also one of the authors of the bestselling SOUL SISTERS AT

CEDAR MOUNTAIN LODGE SERIES, centered around a woman who opens her heart and home to four foster girls one Christmas.

I'm also one of the founding authors of My Book Friends and invite you to join this fun group of readers and authors on Facebook. I'd love to send you my exclusive interview with the canine companions in my Hometown Harbor Series as a thank you for joining my exclusive group of readers. You can sign up by following at my website here: https://www. tammylgrace.com/newsletter

I hope you'll connect with me on social media. You can find me on Facebook, where I have a page and a special group for my readers and follow me on Amazon and BookBub, so you'll know when I have a new release or a deal. Be sure to download the free novella, HOMETOWN HARBOR: THE BEGINNING. It's a prequel to FINDING HOME that I know you'll enjoy.

If you did enjoy this book or any of my other books, I'd be grateful if you took a few minutes to leave a short review on Amazon, BookBub, Goodreads, or any of the other retailers you use.

ABOUT THE AUTHOR

Tammy L. Grace is the *USA Today* bestselling and award-winning author of the Cooper Harrington Detective Novels, the bestselling Hometown Harbor Series, and the Glass Beach Cottage Series, along with several sweet Christmas novellas. Tammy also writes under the pen name of Casey Wilson for Bookouture and Grand Central. You'll find Tammy online at www.tammylgrace.com where you can join her mailing list and be part of her exclusive group of readers. Connect with Tammy on Facebook at www.facebook.com/tammylgrace.books or Instagram at @authortammylgrace.

f facebook.com/tammylgrace.books

🐦 twitter.com/TammyLGrace

📷 instagram.com/authortammylgrace

BB bookbub.com/authors/tammy-l-grace

g goodreads.com/tammylgrace

a amazon.com/author/tammylgrace

Made in the USA
Middletown, DE
20 July 2024

57732550R00149